DECLINE AND FALL

Universities can be full of unexpected dangers. Paul Pennyfeather, a quiet studious young man, has an unfortunate meeting with some drunken party-goers in his college one night. As a result, he is sent down from Oxford for indecent behaviour, and has to take a job as a teacher in a boys' private school.

However, life in Dr Fagan's school in north Wales is not without interest, Paul finds. There is Captain Grimes, with his wooden leg, who seems to lead a rather exciting, if risky, life. There is the anxious Mr Prendergast, who has *Doubts*, and Dr Fagan's two alarming daughters, Florence and Diana (known as Flossie and Dusty by the boys). And who is the mysterious Philbrick, with his diamond tie-pin? Is he Philbrick the school butler, or Sir Solomon Philbrick, the famous author (or ship-owner, or burglar)?

And this is only the beginning of Paul's adventures. On Sports Day, when the parents come to the school, he meets Margot Beste-Chetwynde. She is beautiful, fashionable, charming, enormously rich, and has a mysterious past. And she seems to like Paul, too . . .

OXFORD BOOKWORMS LIBRARY

Human Interest

Decline and Fall

Stage 6 (2500 headwords)

Series Editor: Jennifer Bassett
Founder Editor: Tricia Hedge
Activities Editors: Jennifer Bassett and Alison Baxter

EVELYN WAUGH

Decline and Fall

Retold by
Clare West

OXFORD UNIVERSITY PRESS
2000

OXFORD
UNIVERSITY PRESS

Great Clarendon Street, Oxford OX2 6DP

Oxford University Press is a department of the University of Oxford.
It furthers the University's objective of excellence in research, scholarship,
and education by publishing worldwide in

Oxford New York

Auckland Cape Town Dar es Salaam Hong Kong Karachi
Kuala Lumpur Madrid Melbourne Mexico City Nairobi
New Delhi Shanghai Taipei Toronto

With offices in

Argentina Austria Brazil Chile Czech Republic France Greece
Guatemala Hungary Italy Japan Poland Portugal Singapore
South Korea Switzerland Thailand Turkey Ukraine Vietnam

OXFORD and OXFORD ENGLISH are registered trade marks of
Oxford University Press in the UK and in certain other countries

Illustrated by: Rowan Barnes Murphy

A37556

CONTENTS

PEOPLE IN THIS STORY

Paul Pennyfeather

Mr Sniggs, *Assistant Dean at Scone College*
Mr Postlethwaite, *Domestic Bursar at Scone College*
Sir Alastair Digby-Vane-Trumpington, *a student*
Arthur Potts, *a student and a friend of Paul's*
Mr Levy, *of Church and Stone, educational agents*

Dr Augustus Fagan, *owner of Llanabba Castle School*
Miss Florence Fagan (Flossie) ⎱ *Dr Fagan's daughters*
Miss Diana Fagan (Dusty) ⎰
Captain Grimes, *a teacher*
Mr Prendergast, *a teacher*
Philbrick, *the school butler*
Clutterbuck, *a boy at the school*
Mr and Mrs Clutterbuck, *his parents*
Lord Line, *a boy at the school*
Lord and Lady Circle, *Lord Line's parents*
Peter Beste-Chetwynde, later Lord Pastmaster, *a boy at the school*
Mrs Margot Beste-Chetwynde, *Peter's mother, and a rich, beautiful widow*
Mr Sebastian Cholmondley (Chokey), *Mrs Beste-Chetwynde's lover*

Professor Otto Silenus, *an architect*
Sir Humphrey Maltravers, later Lord Metroland, *a Government Minister*
Sir Wilfred Lucas-Dockery, *a prison governor*

1
PAUL AT OXFORD

Mr Sniggs, the Assistant Dean, and Mr Postlethwaite, the Domestic Bursar, sat alone in Mr Sniggs' room in Scone College. They were the only dons who were at home that evening. Their colleagues were at parties in Oxford, or visiting friends, or attending meetings at other colleges, because it was the night of the annual Bollinger Club dinner – always a difficult time for those responsible for university discipline.

In fact, it is not accurate to call this an annual event, because quite often so much trouble is caused that the Club does not meet again for some years. There is tradition behind the Bollinger; it takes its name from the famous champagne, and past members include men who are now heads of royal families. The last dinner was three years ago. What a wild, destructive night that had been! This was the first meeting since then, and old members had poured into Oxford from all over Europe especially for the occasion – foreign royalty, country gentlemen, Scottish landowners, smooth young businessmen, ambitious lawyers and politicians – to join those who were currently students at this great university.

The party had already started. Mr Postlethwaite and Mr Sniggs could hear the sound of confused shouting and breaking of glass from Sir Alastair Digby-Vane-Trumpington's rooms. They listened eagerly, looking out of the window into the court-yard.

'The fines!' said Mr Sniggs, as he lit his pipe. 'Oh, yes! The fines they'll have to pay after this evening!'

There is some excellent port that is only served to dons when

1

College fines have reached £50. 'We shall have a week of it, at least,' said Mr Postlethwaite. 'A week of College port!'

Louder noises were now coming from Sir Alastair's rooms – a frightening sound for those who have heard it before, the hunting cry of the ancient English families. Soon they would all be rushing into the courtyard, red-faced and shouting, ready for the real fun of the evening.

'Don't you think it might be wiser if we turned off the light?' said Mr Sniggs.

In darkness the two men crept to the window. The courtyard below was already a sea of scarcely recognizable faces.

'There must be fifty of them at least!' said Mr Postlethwaite. 'If only they were all members of the College! Fifty of them at ten pounds each! Oh!'

'It'll be more if they attack the Chapel,' said Mr Sniggs. 'Oh, please God, make them attack the Chapel.'

'I wonder who the unpopular students are this year. The Bollinger always attack their rooms. I hope they've been wise enough to go out for the evening.'

'There's Austen – he has a beautiful piano, I'm told.'

'And Partridge will be another one. I think he collects French paintings.'

'Lord Rending can afford to hunt, but he collects teapots instead.'

'And Sanders has won prizes for his poems, you know.'

'There'll be a heavy bill for tonight, just you see! But I must say I'd feel happier if some of our colleagues were here. The Bollinger can't see us from here, can they?'

It was a lovely evening. They smashed Austen's piano, destroyed Partridge's French paintings, broke Sanders' windows and Rending's teapots. Sir Alastair felt quite ill with excitement, and had to be helped to his bed. It was half-past eleven. Soon the evening would come to an end. But there was still something to look forward to.

⸺◉⸺

Paul Pennyfeather was studying to become a vicar. It was his third year of uneventful residence at Scone College. At school he had been a quiet, hard-working boy, who 'had a good influence on others', according to his reports. Both his parents had died in India when he was young, and so he lived in London with his guardian, a wealthy lawyer, who was proud of Paul's progress and extremely bored by his conversation.

For the last two years Paul had lived carefully on the allowance he received from his guardian. He had no expensive tastes, and very few friends. None of the Bollinger Club had ever heard of Paul Pennyfeather, and he, strangely enough, had not heard of them.

That evening he was walking happily back from a meeting of the League of Nations Union; there had been a most interesting talk on the voting system in Poland. He was planning to smoke a pipe and read a little before going to bed. He entered the College and, in his usual modest, quiet way, started to walk towards his rooms. What a lot of people there were in the courtyard! And they all seemed to be drunk.

Out of the night Lord Lumsden of Strathdrummond appeared, standing unsteadily in Paul's way. Paul tried to pass. Unfortunately, Paul's old school tie, which he was wearing, looked very similar to the Bollinger Club tie. The difference (Paul's tie had a stripe one centimetre wider) was not one that Lumsden of Strathdrummond was likely to appreciate.

'Here's an awful man wearing the Bollinger tie,' said Lord Lumsden. It was easy to see how his family had held control of a large part of Scotland for over two thousand years.

Mr Sniggs was looking anxiously at Mr Postlethwaite. 'I think they've caught somebody,' he said. 'I hope they don't do him any serious harm. Oh dear, can it be Lord Rending? I think I ought to go down there and stop them.'

'No, Sniggs,' said Mr Postlethwaite, laying a warning hand on his hot-headed colleague's arm. 'No, no, no. It would be unwise. We have our position to consider. In their present state they might not listen to reason. We must avoid any unpleasantness for ourselves, at all costs.'

Finally the crowd parted, and Mr Sniggs gave a sigh of relief. 'Oh, it's quite all right. It isn't Rending. It's Pennyfeather – someone of no importance.'

'Well, that saves a lot of trouble. I am glad, Sniggs, I really am. What a lot of clothes that young man appears to have lost!'

'I think they've caught somebody,' said Mr Sniggs.

Next morning there was a lovely College meeting.

'£230,' whispered the Domestic Bursar delightedly to his neighbour at the table, 'not counting the damage! That means five evenings, with what we've already collected. Five evenings of College port!'

'The case of Pennyfeather,' the Dean was saying, 'seems to be quite a different matter. He ran across the courtyard, you say, *without his trousers*. It is not right; in fact, it is indecent. It is certainly not acceptable behaviour.'

'Perhaps if we fined him really heavily?' the Assistant Dean suggested.

'I very much doubt whether he could pay. I understand he is not wealthy. *Without trousers*, indeed! And at that time of night! No, I think we should get rid of him completely. That sort of young man does the College no good at all.'

Two hours later, while Paul was packing his three suits in his little leather case, the Domestic Bursar sent a message that he wished to see him. 'Ah, Mr Pennyfeather,' he said, 'I have examined your rooms and noticed two slight burns on the furniture, no doubt from cigarette-ends. You will pay for this damage before you leave the College. That is all, thank you.'

As he crossed the courtyard, Paul met Mr Sniggs. 'You're just off?' said the Assistant Dean brightly.

'Yes, sir,' said Paul.

A little further on he met the Chaplain. 'Oh, Pennyfeather, before you go, surely you have my copy of Stanley's *Eastern Church*?'

'Yes. I left it on your table.'

'Thank you. Well, goodbye, my dear boy. I suppose that after that terrible business last night, you will have to think of some other profession. You may congratulate yourself that you discovered your unsuitability for the priesthood before it was too late. If a vicar does that sort of thing, you know, all the world knows. And so many do, unfortunately! What are your plans?'

'I don't really know yet.'

'It won't be easy to make a new start. Dear, dear! *No trousers!*'

At the College gates Paul tipped one of the College servants. 'Well, goodbye, Blackall,' he said. 'I don't suppose I shall see you again for some time.'

'No, sir, and very sorry I am to hear it. I expect you'll become a schoolmaster, sir. That's what most of the gentlemen do, sir, who are sent down for indecent behaviour.'

<hr>

'Sent down for indecent behaviour, eh?' said Paul's guardian. 'Thank God your poor father will never know about this. That's all I can say.' There was a short silence.

'Well,' he went on, 'you know how your father left his money. You will receive five thousand pounds on your twenty-first birthday, in eleven months' time. The allowance I've been paying you comes from the interest on that money. As you know, I am instructed by him to stop your allowance at any time, if your education comes to an end, or if I consider your way of life unsatisfactory. Your poor father trusted me, and I must do what he would wish. So I will not be continuing your allowance. Moreover, I am sure you will realize how impossible it would be for you to share the same home with my daughter.'

'But what should I do?' said Paul.

'I think you ought to find some work,' said his guardian.

'But what kind of work?'

'Just good, healthy work. Your life has been rather too

comfortable up to now, Paul. Perhaps I am to blame for that. It will do you the world of good to see what life is really like.'

'Have I no legal right to any money at all?' asked Paul.

'None whatever, my dear boy,' said his guardian cheerfully.

That spring Paul's guardian's daughter had two new evening dresses, and as a result, became engaged to a well-behaved young man who worked in a government office.

———◆———

'Sent down for indecent behaviour, eh?' said Mr Levy, of Church and Stone, educational agents. 'Well, I don't think we'll say anything about that. We call that "Education discontinued for personal reasons". I think we have just the job for you. What about this?' He passed an advertisement to Paul, who read:

SCHOOLMASTER REQUIRED IMMEDIATELY

To teach English, Maths, German and French at Llanabba Castle School, North Wales. Experience essential; excellent sports teaching essential. £120 resident post. Reply to Dr Augustus Fagan, with copies of references and photographs, if considered advisable.

'Perfect for you,' said Mr Levy.

'But I don't know a word of German, I've had no experience, I've got no references, and I can't play any sport.'

'You shouldn't be too modest,' said Mr Levy. 'It's wonderful what people can teach when they try. Anyway, Dr Fagan can't expect *all* that for the salary he's offering. Between ourselves, Llanabba hasn't a good name in the profession – it's in the group we call School. We put schools, you see, into four groups: Leading School, First-class School, Good School, and School. To be honest,' said Mr Levy, 'School is pretty bad. I think you'll find it a very suitable post. As far as I know, there are only two

7

other candidates, and one of them is totally deaf, poor man.'

Next day Paul returned to Church and Stone to meet Dr Fagan, who was already interviewing the other candidates. After a few minutes Mr Levy called Paul into a room, introduced him to Dr Fagan, and then left them alone together.

'Most exhausting,' said Dr Fagan. 'I am sure he was a very nice young man, but I couldn't make him understand a word I said. Can *you* hear me quite clearly?'

'Perfectly, thank you.'

'Good.' Dr Fagan was very tall, very old and very well-dressed, with sunken eyes and rather long white hair over black eyebrows. 'Now, I understand that you have had no experience? Of course, that is in many ways an advantage. The older professional teacher so easily loses imagination, vision! But we must be sensible. I am offering a salary of £120, but only to a man with experience. I understand, too, that you left your university rather suddenly. Now, why was that?'

This was the question Paul had been nervously expecting, and he had decided to tell the truth. 'I was sent down, sir, for indecent behaviour.'

'Indeed, indeed? Well, I shall not ask for details. I have been in the teaching profession for long enough to know that nobody enters it unless he has some very good reason which he is anxious to hide. But you see, Mr Pennyfeather, I cannot pay £120 to anyone who has been sent down for indecent behaviour. Suppose we fix your salary at £90 a year to begin with? I shall expect you tomorrow evening. There is an excellent train that leaves London at about ten. I think you will like your work,' he continued dreamily. 'You will find my school is built upon an ideal – an ideal of service and trust. Many of the boys come from the very best families.' Dr Fagan gave a long sigh. 'I wish I could say the same for the masters. Between ourselves, Pennyfeather, I think I shall have to get rid of Grimes quite soon.' He stood up, and put his hat on. 'Goodbye, my dear Pennyfeather. I think, in fact I know, that we are going to work well together. I can always tell these things.'

'Goodbye, sir,' said Paul.

'You owe me five per cent of £90,' said Mr Levy cheerfully. 'You can pay me now or later.'

'I'll pay you when I get my wages,' said Paul.

'Just as you please. Glad to have been of use to you.'

2
LLANABBA CASTLE SCHOOL

From the back, Llanabba Castle looks very much like any other large country house, with a great many windows, a chain of glasshouses, and the roofs of several kitchen buildings disappearing into the trees. But from the front, and that is how it is approached from Llanabba station, it looks just like a castle. Visitors have to drive past at least a kilometre of forbiddingly high stone walls to reach the school, which stands square and solid, protected by ancient-looking towers to east and west.

Driving up from the station in a taxi, Paul saw little of all this. It was almost dark by the time he arrived.

'I am Mr Pennyfeather,' he said to the butler. 'I have come here as a master.'

'Yes,' said the butler. 'I know all about you. This way.'

They went down a number of passages, unlit and smelling of the awful smells of school, until they reached a door. 'In there.

That's the Masters' Common Room.' And without another word, the butler disappeared into the darkness.

Paul looked round. All his life he had been used to living in small spaces, but even to him this room did not seem large. There were all sorts of things here – sixteen pipes on a shelf, a walking stick and an umbrella in a corner, a typewriter, some very old books, yesterday's *Daily News* and half a bottle of cheap port on the table. He sat down miserably on a chair.

Soon there was a knock on the door, and a small boy came in. 'Oh!' he said, looking interestedly at Paul.

'Hullo!' said Paul.

'I was looking for Captain Grimes,' said the little boy.

'Oh!' said Paul.

'I suppose you're the new master?' said the child.

'Yes,' said Paul. 'I'm called Pennyfeather.'

The little boy gave a shout of laughter, and went away.

During the next half hour, eight or nine boys appeared, giving various excuses, and stared at Paul. Then a bell rang, and there was a loud noise of whistling and running outside. The door opened again, and a very short man of about thirty came into the Common Room. He had an artificial leg, and a short red moustache, and was slightly bald.

'Hullo!' he said. 'I'm Captain Grimes.' Then he added to someone outside, 'Come in, you.' Another boy came in. 'Why did you whistle,' said Grimes, 'when I told you to stop?'

'Everyone else was whistling,' said the boy.

'What's that got to do with it?' said Grimes.

'I should think it had a lot to do with it,' said the boy.

'Well, just you write out a hundred times, "I must not whistle", and next time, remember, I shall beat you,' said

Grimes. 'With this,' he went on, waving the walking stick.

'That wouldn't hurt much,' said the boy, and went out.

'There's no discipline in the place,' said Grimes, and then he went out too.

'I wonder whether I'm going to enjoy being a schoolmaster,' thought Paul.

Soon another and older man came in. 'Hullo!' he said. 'I'm Prendergast. Have some port?'

'Thank you, I'd love to.'

'Well, there's only one glass.'

'Oh, well, it doesn't matter, then.'

'Perhaps we'll have some another night. I suppose you're the new master?'

'Yes.'

'You'll hate it here. I know. I've been here ten years. Grimes only came this term. He hates it already. He isn't a gentleman, of course. By the way, those are my pipes on the shelf. Remind me to show them to you after dinner.'

At this moment the butler appeared with a message that Dr Fagan wished to see Mr Pennyfeather.

Dr Fagan's part of the Castle was considerably more spacious and comfortable. Wearing expensive evening clothes, he greeted Paul casually. Sitting in front of the fire was a brightly dressed woman of about forty. 'That,' said Dr Fagan with some disgust, 'is my daughter.'

'Pleased to meet you,' said Miss Fagan. 'Now what I always tell the young men is, "Don't let the dad overwork you." He loves work, does Dad. But he can be – inhuman. Can't you?' she added, turning on her father with sudden fierceness.

'At times, my dear, I am grateful for any distance between

11

myself and humankind. But here,' he added, 'is my other daughter.' Silently, another woman had entered the room, with a bunch of keys on her belt. She was younger than her sister, but far less cheerful.

'How do you do?' she said. 'I do hope you have brought some soap with you. Masters are not provided with soap or towels. Do you take sugar in your tea?'

'Yes, usually.'

'I will make a note of that, and have two extra lumps put out for you. But don't let the boys get them.'

'I have put you in charge of the fifth year for the rest of this term,' said Dr Fagan. 'You will find them delightful boys, quite delightful. Keep an eye on Clutterbuck, by the way, a very delicate little chap. I have also put you in charge of sports, woodwork and the fire practice. And do you teach music?'

'No, I'm afraid not.'

'Unfortunate, most unfortunate. I understood from Mr Levy that you did. I have arranged for you to take Beste-Chetwynde in organ lessons twice a week. Well, you must do the best you can. There goes the bell for dinner. I won't keep you. Oh, one other thing. Not a word to the boys, please, about the reasons for your leaving Oxford! We schoolmasters have to choose our words carefully. Occasionally we even have to deceive the young people in our care. There, I think I have said something for you to think about. Good night.'

'Bye, bye,' said the elder Miss Fagan brightly.

Paul was guided to the dining-hall by the smell of cooking and the sound of voices. There were fifty or sixty boys, between ten and eighteen years old, sitting around four long tables. Paul sat down at the head of one of the tables, next to the boy who had

whistled at Captain Grimes. Paul thought he rather liked him.
'I'm called Beste-Chetwynde,' the boy said.

'I've got to teach you the organ, I believe.'

'Yes, it's great fun. We play in the village church. Do you play
terribly well?'

Remembering Dr Fagan's advice, Paul said, 'Yes, remarkably
well.'

'Well, you won't be able to teach me much,' said Beste-
Chetwynde cheerfully. 'I only do it to get out of football. I say,
they haven't given you a knife. These servants are too awful.
Philbrick,' he shouted to the butler, 'go and get a knife for Mr
Pennyfeather at once. That man's all right, really,' he added,
'only you need to watch him.'

In a few minutes Philbrick returned with the knife.

'It seems to me you're a remarkably intelligent boy,' said Paul.

'Captain Grimes says I'm stupid. I'm glad you're not like
Captain Grimes. He's so common, don't you think?'

'You mustn't talk about the other masters like that in front of
me.'

The boy on Paul's other side spoke for the first time. 'Mr
Prendergast wears a wig,' he said, and then laughed quietly.

All this was much easier than Paul had expected. It didn't
seem so very hard to get on with boys, after all.

After dinner, Captain Grimes came up to him, and put a hand
on his shoulder. 'Awful meal, wasn't it, old boy?'

'Pretty bad,' said Paul.

'Prendy – you've met Prendergast, haven't you? – is on duty
tonight. I'm off to the pub. How about you?'

'All right,' said Paul.

'Prendy's all right in his way,' said Grimes, 'but he can't keep control of the boys. Very hard for a man with a wig to keep control. I've got a false leg, but that's different. Boys respect that. They think I lost it in the war. Actually, just between ourselves, it was when I got rather drunk one night in Stoke-on-Trent, and was run down by a bus. But it's not a good idea to tell everyone

'Awful meal, wasn't it, old boy?' said Grimes.

about that. Funny thing, but I feel I can trust you. I think we're going to be good friends.'

'I hope so,' said Paul.

'Have you met Miss Fagan?'

'I've met two.'

'They're both awful,' said Grimes, and added gloomily, 'I'm engaged to be married to Flossie.'

'Good God! Which is she?'

'The elder. Their names are Florence and Diana, but the boys call them Flossie and Dusty. We haven't told the old man yet. I'm waiting till I land in the soup again. Then I shall play that as my last card. I usually get into the soup sooner or later. Here's the pub. The beer's not bad.'

In the corner of the bar sat the butler, Philbrick, talking in Welsh to an elderly man who Paul recognized as the station-master. As they started drinking their beer, Grimes sighed happily. 'This looks like being the first end of term I've seen for two years,' he said dreamily. 'Funny thing, I can always manage all right for about six weeks, and then I land in the soup. I don't believe I was ever meant by Nature to be a schoolmaster. My character,' said Grimes, with a faraway look in his eyes – 'that's been my trouble, my character and sex.'

'Is it quite easy to get another job after – after you've been in the soup?' asked Paul.

'Not at first, it isn't, but there are ways. Besides, you see, I'm a public-school man. That means everything. There's a wonderful fairness in the English social system,' said Grimes, 'that makes sure the public-school man will never starve. You go through four or five years of perfect hell at an age when life is certain to be hell anyway, and after that the social system never lets you down. Actually I didn't manage four or five years of it; they asked me to leave soon after my sixteenth birthday. But my headmaster was a public-school man. "Grimes," he said, "I can't keep you in the school after what has happened. But I want you to be able to start again." So he wrote me a letter of recommendation to any future employer, a really good letter, too. I've still got it. It's been very useful at one time or another. That's the public-school system, you see. They may force you to leave, but they never let you down.

'After that I went into business. And then the war started. You're too young to have been in the war, I suppose? Those were the days, old boy. It'll never be like that again. I think I was probably drunk for almost the whole of that war. Then I got into the soup again, pretty badly that time. They said, "Now, Grimes, you've got to behave like a gentleman. We don't want one of our officers involved in a court case. We're going to leave you alone for half an hour. There's your gun. You know what to do. Goodbye, old man," they said quite warmly. Well, I put the gun to my head twice, but each time I brought it down again. "Public-school men don't end like this," I said to myself. It was a long half-hour, but luckily they'd left a bottle of whisky in there with me. There wasn't much left when they came back. They looked so surprised, and disgusted, seeing me alive and drunk, that all I could do was laugh. Well, they arranged a trial, but the officer who was supposed to be the judge had been at school with me! So he managed to send me off to Ireland to do some nice easy little job for the rest of the war. You can't get into the soup in Ireland, however hard you try. I don't know if you find this boring?'

'Not at all,' said Paul. 'I think it's most encouraging.'

Just then Philbrick approached them. 'Feeling lonely?' he

said. 'I've been talking to the station-master, and if either of you wants an introduction to a young lady—'

'Certainly not,' said Paul.

'Oh, all right,' said Philbrick, departing.

'Women are a mystery,' said Grimes, 'as far as Grimes is concerned.'

Next morning Paul was woken by a loud bang on his door, and Beste-Chetwynde looked in. 'Good morning, sir,' he said. 'I thought I'd tell you, there's only one bathroom for the masters, and if you want to get there before Mr Prendergast, you should go now. Captain Grimes doesn't wash much.'

Paul went to the bathroom. A few minutes later he was rewarded by hearing someone approaching and trying desperately to open the door. After breakfast Paul went to the Common Room, where he found Mr Prendergast.

'I suppose I shall have to find some other time for my bath,' said Mr Prendergast sadly. 'Oh dear! I can see things are going to be very difficult.'

'But surely we could both have one?'

'No, no, that's out of the question. It's all part of the same thing. Everything's been like this since I left the Church. If things had happened differently, I'd be a vicar now, with my own little house and bathroom. Only' – and Mr Prendergast dropped his voice to a whisper – 'only I had *Doubts*. I don't know why I'm telling you all this, nobody else knows, but I somehow feel you'll understand. Ten years ago, I was a vicar in the Church of England. I had such an attractive church, not old, but *very* beautiful, with an excellent heating system. As soon as I moved into the house, my mother came to look after me. She bought some material, with her own money, for the sitting-room curtains, and she used to invite the ladies of the village to tea one afternoon a week. It was all very pleasant until my *Doubts* began.'

'Were they as bad as all that?' asked Paul politely.

'They couldn't have been worse; that is why I am here today. My mother had made friends with a charming couple called Bundle, and we were having supper with them one evening, when suddenly, for no reason at all, my *Doubts* began.'

He paused, and Paul felt obliged to offer some expression of sympathy. 'What a terrible thing!' he said.

'Yes, I've not known an hour's real happiness since then. You see, it's so basic. *I couldn't understand why God had made the world at all*. And so I really felt I had to resign my post and give up the idea of being a vicar. It was a great shock for my poor mother, especially after she had bought the curtain material and got so friendly with the Bundles.'

A bell rang down a distant passage. He sighed. 'Well, perhaps one day I'll see the Light, and then I'll go back to the Church. Meanwhile—'

A boy ran past the door, whistling horribly.

'That's Clutterbuck,' said Mr Prendergast. 'A nasty little boy, if ever there was one.'

3
DISCIPLINE

All the boys and masters were required to attend prayers, which were held in the main hall after breakfast every day. When Paul arrived, he found the boys standing in rows, waiting for Dr Fagan, while Grimes was sitting on a chair.

'Morning,' he said to Paul. 'I've only just got up, I'm afraid. Do I smell of drink?'

'Yes,' said Paul.

'That's because I missed breakfast. Has Prendy been telling you about his Doubts?'

'Yes,' said Paul.

'Funny thing,' said Grimes, 'but I've never been worried in that way. I don't pretend to be a particularly religious man, but I've never had any Doubts. When you've been in the soup as often as I have, it gives you a sort of feeling that everything will be all right in the end. I don't believe you can ever be unhappy for long, provided you do exactly what you want to and when you want to. Ah, here comes the old man.'

The masters stood up as Dr Fagan walked quickly into the hall, and the service began. After a reading and a prayer, the Doctor looked at a sheet of notes he was holding in his hand. 'Boys,' he said, 'I have some announcements to make. This year the Fagan challenge cup for running will not be competed for, because of the floods.'

'I expect the old boy has sold it,' said Grimes in Paul's ear. 'Silver, you know.'

'Nor will the Llanabba Writing Prize.'

'Because of the floods,' whispered Grimes.

'I have received my telephone bill,' continued the Doctor, 'and I find that during the past three months there have been no fewer than twenty-three long-distance calls to London, none of which has been made by myself or anyone in my family. This must stop immediately. And one other thing – Boys, I have been deeply saddened to learn that several cigar ends have been found in the boot-room. I consider this an extremely serious matter. What boy has been smoking cigars in the boot-room?'

There was a long silence, during which the Doctor's eye travelled down the line of boys. 'I will give the guilty boy until lunch-time to confess. If I do not hear from him by then, the whole school will be punished.'

'Hell!' said Grimes. 'I gave those cigars to Clutterbuck. I hope the little devil has the sense to keep quiet.'

Prayers were now over, and the boys left the hall to go to their classrooms. Grimes pointed to a door. 'That's your little gang in there,' he told Paul. 'You let them out at eleven.'

'But what am I to teach them?' said Paul in sudden panic.

'Oh, I wouldn't try to *teach* them anything, not just yet, anyway. Just keep them quiet.'

'Now that's a thing I've never learned to do,' sighed Mr Prendergast. Paul watched him walk into his classroom, where a burst of clapping greeted his arrival. Dumb with terror, Paul went into his own classroom. Ten boys sat there, their hands folded, their eyes bright with interest.

'Good morning, sir,' said one.

'Good morning,' said Paul.

'Good morning, sir,' said the next.

'Good morning,' said Paul.

'Good morning, sir,' said another.

'Oh, shut up,' said Paul. At this, the boy began to cry quietly, and the others all called out loudly, 'Oh, sir, you've hurt his feelings. He's very sensitive. It's his Welsh blood, you know. Say "good morning" to him, sir, or he won't be happy all day. After all, it *is* a good morning, isn't it, sir?'

'Silence!' shouted Paul, and for a few moments things were quieter.

'Please, sir,' said one, 'please, sir, perhaps he's been smoking cigars and doesn't feel well.'

'Silence!' said Paul again. The ten boys stopped talking, and sat perfectly still, staring at him. He felt himself getting hot and red. 'I suppose the first thing is to get your names clear. What is your name?' he asked, turning to the first boy.

'Line, sir.'

'And yours?'

'Line, sir,' said the next boy. Paul's heart sank.

'But you can't both be called Line.'

'No, sir, *I'm* Line. He's just trying to be funny.'

'*Me* trying to be funny! Please, sir, I'm Line, really I am.'

'Well, if it comes to that,' said Clutterbuck, 'there's only one Line here, and that's me. Anyone else can go to hell.'

Paul felt desperate. 'Is there anyone who *isn't* Line?'

Four or five voices were instantly heard. 'I'm not, sir, I wouldn't be called Line, not even if you paid me, sir.' In a few seconds the room had become divided into two groups, those who were Line and those who were not. Fighting had already started, when the door opened and Grimes came in.

'I thought you might want this,' he said, handing Paul a walking stick. 'Take my advice and give them some work to do.'

He went out, and Paul, holding the stick firmly, faced up to his class. 'Listen,' he said, 'I don't care what any of you are called, but if there's another word from anyone, I'll keep you all in this afternoon. Now you will all write as much as you can on "Selfishness". There will be a prize of half a crown for the boy who writes the most.'

From then onwards, there was silence until the break. By the time the bell rang for the end of the lesson, Clutterbuck had written sixteen pages, and was given the half-crown.

'Did you find those boys difficult to manage?' asked Mr Prendergast, filling his pipe.

'Not at all,' said Paul.

'Ah, you're lucky. I find all boys completely impossible to control. Of course my wig has a lot to do with it. Have you noticed I wear a wig?'

'No, no, of course not.'

'Well, the boys did as soon as they saw it. I should never have got one. You see, I thought when I left my last post that I looked too old to get a job easily. I knew immediately that it was a mistake, but by the time the boys had seen it, it was too late to stop wearing it. They make all sorts of jokes about it.'

'I expect they'd laugh at something else if it wasn't that.'

'Yes, no doubt they would. Oh dear! If I didn't have my pipes, I don't know how I could keep going. What made you come here?'

'I was sent down from Oxford for indecent behaviour.'

'Oh yes, like Grimes?'

'No,' said Paul firmly, 'not like Grimes.'

'Oh, well, it's all much the same really.'

Two days later Beste-Chetwynde was practising on the organ in the village church. It was his second music lesson with Paul.

'Do you know, sir, the fifth year really rather like you?'

'Is that so unusual?' asked Paul. 'Stop playing for a moment, can't you?'

'Very few masters get on with them,' said Beste-Chetwynde. 'And I'll tell you another thing. You know that man Philbrick. There's something strange about him.'

'I've no doubt of it.'

'It's not just that he's such a bad butler. The servants are always awful here. But he has a great big diamond ring, and says he used to eat off gold plates. *We* believe he isn't a butler at all, but a member of a foreign royal family, hiding in England until the political situation improves in his country.'

'He looks very English to me.'

'Well, that's what we think, anyway. And now I *am* going to play the organ. After all, my mother does pay five pounds a term extra for me to learn.'

———————

At the end of the week, as Paul sat in the Common Room waiting for the bell for tea, he found himself thinking that on the whole things had not been quite as awful as he had expected. As Beste-Chetwynde had told him, he was a distinct success with his class. After the first day they had come to an unspoken agreement. When Paul wished to read or write letters, the boys did not disturb him; when he decided it was time to talk to them about their lessons, they remained silent; and when he gave them homework to do, some of it was done. It had rained every day, so there had been no games. No punishments, no problems, no effort, and in the evenings the confessions of Grimes, which provided material for a fascinating study of shamelessness.

Mr Prendergast came in with the post. 'A letter for you, two for Grimes,' he said. 'No one ever writes to me. When I was a vicar, I used to get five or six letters a day. Grimes' letters look like bills. *I* always pay cash, or I would if I ever bought anything. The last thing I bought was that walking stick. Grimes uses it for beating the boys with. I hadn't really meant to buy one, but I went into a shop to ask for some tobacco, and they hadn't got the

When Paul wished to read or write letters, the boys did not disturb him.

sort I wanted. I felt I couldn't leave without getting something, so I bought that. It cost half a crown,' he added sadly, 'so I couldn't afford any tea that day.'

Paul took his letter. It was from one of his few friends in Oxford, the solid, reliable Arthur Potts.

Scone College, Oxford

My dear Pennyfeather,

I need hardly tell you how unhappy I was to hear of your terrible misfortune. It seems to me that a real injustice has been done to you. A very strange thing happened last night. I was just going to bed when Digby-Vane-Trumpington came into my room without knocking. As you know, I had never spoken to him before. He told me he wanted to apologize to you for getting you into such a mess, as he called it, and then he offered – you will never believe this! – to send you some money as a sort of apology!

He mentioned £20. As you can imagine, I told him what I thought of him for making such an insulting suggestion. I asked him how he dared treat a gentleman like that. He seemed rather surprised, and went away.

I discovered an interesting little church in the village of Little Bechley yesterday, and wished you had been with me.

Yours,

Arthur Potts

P.S. I understand you are thinking of taking up educational work. It seems to me that the great problem of education is to train young minds to choose between right and wrong, not just to learn self-control. I shall be interested to hear what your experience of this has been.

'What do you think about that?' asked Paul, handing Mr Prendergast the letter.

'Well,' he said, after studying it carefully, 'I think your friend is wrong. People should never rely on their *own* opinions and feelings, should they?'

'No, I mean about the money.'

'My dear Pennyfeather! I hope you are in no doubt about that. Accept it at once! It would be wicked to refuse. Twenty pounds! Why, it takes me half a term to earn that.'

The bell rang for tea. In the dining-hall Paul showed the letter to Grimes. 'Should I take the twenty pounds?' he asked.

'Take it? My God! Of course you should.'

'Well, I'm not sure,' said Paul. He thought about it all the rest of the afternoon and evening, until finally he made up his mind. It was a hard struggle, but his early training was victorious. He tried to explain something of what he felt to Grimes as they sat in the pub that evening.

'I'm afraid you'll find my attitude rather hard to understand,' he said. 'There's every reason why I should take this money. Digby-Vane-Trumpington is extremely rich. Because of him and his friends I have suffered terribly. My whole future is ruined, and I have lost my guardian's allowance. An ordinary person would consider the money justly mine. But,' said Paul, 'I am a gentleman. I can't help it. I was born one; it's in my blood. I simply can't take that money. It would be a betrayal of everything I believe in.'

'Well, I'm a gentleman too, old boy,' said Grimes, 'and I was afraid you might feel like that, so I did my best for you and saved you from yourself.'

'What do you mean by that?'

'Dear old boy, don't be angry, but immediately after tea I sent a telegram to your friend Potts, saying *Tell Trumpington send money quick* and I signed it *Pennyfeather*.'

'Grimes, how awful of you!' said Paul, but he felt a great wave of satisfaction rise up within him. 'We must have another drink on that. Let's drink to the permanence of ideals!'

'My God, what a mouthful!' said Grimes. 'Much too long for me to say. Your very good health!'

Two days later came another letter from Arthur Potts:

Dear Pennyfeather,

Here is Trumpington's cheque for £20. I am glad I shall not have to see him again. I cannot pretend to understand your attitude in this matter, but no doubt you are the best judge.

Yours,

Arthur Potts

P.S. There is a most interesting article in the Educational Review *on the new ideas introduced at the Innesborough High School.*

Apparently teachers there put small objects into the children's mouths, and make them draw the shapes they can feel. Have you tried this with your boys? I must say I do envy you your opportunities.

'How about a party?' said Grimes, when he heard that the cheque had arrived.

'Yes,' said Paul, 'I'd like to ask Prendy too.'

'Why, of course. It's just what he needs. He's been looking very miserable lately. Why don't we all go over to the Metropole at Cwmpryddyg for dinner one night next week?'

Later in the day Paul suggested it to Mr Prendergast.

'Really, Pennyfeather! That's extremely kind of you. I can't remember when I last had dinner at a hotel. Certainly not since the war. My dear boy, I hardly know what to say.'

And much to Paul's embarrassment, a tear appeared in each of Mr Prendergast's eyes and rolled slowly down his face.

4
THE SPORTS DAY

That day was the first without rain, and by half-past one the sun was shining. At lunch-time the Doctor made one of his rare visits to the dining-hall.

'Boys,' he said in a fatherly manner, 'I have an announcement to make. Clutterbuck, will you kindly stop eating while I am speaking. The boys' manners need correcting, Mr Prendergast. Boys, the main sporting event of the year, the Annual School Sports, will take place in the playing-fields tomorrow. Mr Pennyfeather, who, as you know, is himself a distinguished sportsman, will be in charge of all arrangements. Some races will be held today, and the winners will compete in tomorrow's events. Lady Circle has kindly agreed to present the prizes, and I shall myself attend the Sports tomorrow. That is all, thank you. Mr Pennyfeather, perhaps you will be kind enough to spare me a few moments of your time after lunch?'

'Good God!' murmured Paul. When he went to Dr Fagan's sitting-room a little later, he found the Doctor highly excited.

'Ah, come in, Pennyfeather! I am just about to make the arrangements for tomorrow. Florence, will you phone the Clutterbucks and some of the other parents, to invite them. The more guests, the better! And Diana, for the tea we will need sandwiches and cakes, plenty of cakes. Philbrick, there must be champagne-cup – you know, champagne mixed with fruit juice – and will you also help the men to put up the tea-tent. And flags, Diana! I expect there are flags left over from last time.'

'I used them as cleaning cloths,' said Dusty.

'Well, we must buy more. No expense must be spared. Pennyfeather, as soon as you have the results of today's races, telephone them to the printers, and they will have the programmes ready by tomorrow. And there must be flowers, Diana, heaps of flowers,' said the Doctor enthusiastically. 'Do you think we should present Lady Circle with some flowers?'

'No,' said Dusty.

'Nonsense!' said the Doctor. 'It is rarely that the studious calm of Llanabba is taken over by the spirit of celebration, but when it happens, then taste and sensitivity must be shown. You will produce the most expensive arrangement of flowers that Wales can offer. Flowers, youth, wisdom, sunlight falling on jewellery, music,' said the Doctor, his imagination running wild, 'music! There must be a band.'

'I never heard of such a thing,' said Dusty. 'A band indeed! You'll be having fireworks next.'

'*And fireworks*!' said the Doctor, 'and do you think we should buy Mr Prendergast a new tie?'

'No,' said Dusty firmly, 'that is going too far. Flowers and fireworks are one thing, but we must stop somewhere. It would be wasteful and wrong to buy Mr Prendergast a tie.'

'Perhaps you are right,' said the Doctor. 'But we must have music. Will you contact the Llanabba Silver Band, Florence? I hear they have recently won a third prize for their playing. I think the station-master is their leader. And we must ask the *Llandudno News* to send a photographer. Will you give him some whisky, Philbrick? I remember on one of our previous sports days I forgot to offer the reporter any whisky, and the result was a *most* unfortunate photograph. He should never have been allowed into the boys' changing room with his camera. And Pennyfeather, I hope you will make sure that the prizes are distributed fairly evenly about the school. It isn't sensible to let any boy win more than two events; I leave you to arrange that. I think it would be only right if little Lord Line won something. After all, his mother is presenting the prizes! And Beste-Chetwynde – yes, his mother will be here too. I am afraid all this has been thrown upon your shoulders rather suddenly. I only learnt this morning that Lady Circle intended to visit us, and as Mrs Beste-Chetwynde was coming too, it seemed too good an opportunity to miss. She's Lord Pastmaster's sister-in-law, you know – a very wealthy woman, and South American. People say she poisoned her husband, but of course little Beste-Chetwynde doesn't know that. It never came to court, but there was a great deal of talk about it at the time. Perhaps you remember the case?'

'No,' said Paul.

'Powdered glass,' said Flossie in her high voice.

'In strong black coffee,' said Dusty.

'To work!' said the Doctor. 'We have a lot to do.'

It was raining again by the time Paul and Mr Prendergast reached the playing-fields. The boys were waiting for them in miserable little groups, looking cold and wet.

'How shall we organize the races?' asked Paul.

'I don't know,' said Mr Prendergast gloomily. 'I hate the whole business. Oh dear, oh dear, how wet I'm getting.'

'Please, sir,' said Beste-Chetwynde, 'we're all getting rather cold. We could run our races in small groups.'

'All right. Get into four groups. Prendy,' added Paul, 'will you look after them? Philbrick and I will try to find some equipment for the jumping.'

'I'll try,' said Mr Prendergast sadly.

Paul and Philbrick went back to the school buildings.

'Of course,' said Philbrick, 'I shouldn't really be anyone's servant. I expect you wonder how I come to be here?'

'No,' said Paul firmly. 'I don't in the least want to hear about it. I don't want to hear your hateful confessions.'

'It isn't a hateful confession. It's a love-story, in fact – the most beautiful story. You've heard of Sir Solomon Philbrick?'

'No,' said Paul.

'What, never heard of him? Well, that's me. And I can tell you, it's a pretty famous name in London, south of the river. Of course I'm not "Sir" really – people just call me that because they respect me, see? Ever heard of "Chick" Philbrick? No, I suppose he was before your time. Useful little boxer he was, although he drank too much. He was my dad, a good-hearted sort of man, but rough. He used to beat my poor mother a lot, and was sent to prison for it twice. There aren't many like him nowadays – education and whisky are too expensive. Well, Chick got me a job selling tickets for the boxing on Saturday nights. It was there I met Toby Cruttwell. Heard of him?'

'No, I'm terribly afraid I don't know any sportsmen.'

'Sportsmen! Don't make me laugh! Toby Cruttwell, who organized the Buller diamond robbery of 1912 and the Royal Bank robberies of 1910 and 1914? Nobody would call him a sportsman. Well, he and I worked together for five years, and we made a nice little profit. When I retired from crime, I used my share to buy a pub, the *Lamb and Flag* in south London. It was a comfortable life – my wife managed the pub for me. But when she died after the war, I couldn't decide what to do next. I used to lie awake, thinking of the old times, and I felt I needed more excitement in my life. Well, one Saturday night I was in my pub, when I met a man, Jimmy Drage. I used to know him when I was working with Toby. He told me he'd just been involved in an attempted kidnapping that had failed completely. When I told him what he should have done to make the plan succeed, he got quite annoyed and challenged me to do better. Well, I was delighted to have the chance of using my intelligence for a change, so I accepted the challenge. Together we opened the newspaper, to find a victim, and it fell open at a picture of Lady Circle with her only son Lord Line. "There's your boy," said Jimmy. And that's what brought me here.'

'But, my God!' said Paul. 'Why have you told me this terrible story? I shall certainly inform the police.'

'That's all right,' said Philbrick. 'There won't be any kidnapping. All this was before I met Dina, see? Miss Diana to you. The moment I saw that girl, my heart just stood still. That girl could bring a man up from the depths of hell itself.'

'You feel as strongly as that about her?'

'I'd go through fire and water for that girl. She's not happy here. I don't think her dad treats her well. Sometimes I think she's only marrying me to get away from here.'

'Good God! Are you going to get married?'

'We arranged it last Thursday. We've been seeing each other for some time. Then, when she heard that I owned a pub, that made her think I was a bit more than just a butler. It was she who actually suggested our getting married. She's a real business-woman, she is. Just what I need at the *Lamb*. Love's a wonderful thing.' Philbrick stopped speaking, evidently deeply moved by his story.

The door opened, and Mr Prendergast came in.

'Well,' said Paul, 'how are the races going?'

'Not very well,' said Mr Prendergast, 'in fact, they've gone. You see, none of the boys came back from any of the races. They probably just went indoors to change. You can't blame them. It's terribly cold. But it's discouraging, you know, when you keep sending them off and none come back.'

They found Grimes in the Common Room. 'You leave this to me,' he said. 'I've been in this business some time.' In a few minutes he had written down a list of names.

'Clutterbuck seems to have done well,' said Paul.

'Yes, he's a wonderful little runner. Now just phone that to the printers, and the programmes will be ready tomorrow.'

Fortunately, it did not rain the next day, and after morning lessons, everybody appeared, dressed in their best clothes. While Captain Grimes and Mr Prendergast went out to the pub 'for a quick one', Paul discussed the arrangements with Dr Fagan.

'You know,' said the Doctor, 'I find it hard to understand my present excitement. No entertainment fills me with greater horror than a sports display, and the two women in the world whose company I am least able to bear are Mrs Beste-Chetwynde and Lady Circle. Moreover, I have just had an extremely unpleasant conversation with my butler, who – will you believe it? – insisted on wearing a bright yellow sports jacket and diamond tie-pin while serving lunch. And I must confess that all the sports days we have had at Llanabba up to now have been, in one way or another, complete failures. But I still look forward to each new disaster with the greatest delight. Perhaps, Pennyfeather, you will bring luck to Llanabba.'

They walked to the playing-fields, where a large tea-tent was in position. Inside, Dusty was arranging plates of highly coloured cakes on a table, while two servants were cutting sandwiches. 'Remember, Mr Pennyfeather,' said Dusty, 'the champagne-cup is *not* for the masters. You'd better tell Captain Grimes that, too. Mr Prendergast would not think of having any.'

'The guests' cars will be parked just outside the tent,' said the Doctor. 'It will give a pleasant background to the photographs. Pennyfeather, could you guide the photographer in the direction of Mrs Beste-Chetwynde's Rolls Royce, rather than Lady Circle's little car. All these things are important.'

'I'm afraid we can't find any equipment for the long-jump, high-jump, weight-lifting or hammer-throwing,' said Paul.

'We will say these events have already taken place,' said the Doctor smoothly. 'Anything else?'

'The men haven't marked the ground out for the races.'

'Just judge the distance by eye. Really, my dear Pennyfeather, it is quite unlike you to create difficulties like this. Let them go on racing until it is time for tea, and remember,' he added wisely, 'the longer the race, the more time it takes. I leave the details to you. I am more interested in giving the right *impression*. I wish, for example, that we had a starting-pistol.'

'Would this be any use?' said Philbrick, producing an enormous army pistol. 'Be careful – it has bullets in it.'

'Just what we need,' said the Doctor. 'But fire into the ground, remember. We must do everything we can to avoid an accident. Do you always carry that around with you?'

'Only when I'm wearing my diamonds,' said Philbrick.

'Well, I hope that is not often. Good God! Who are these extraordinary-looking people?'

Ten men of disgusting appearance were approaching. They were small and dark, with bent backs, tiny bright eyes and long, monkey-like arms.

'Madmen!' cried Philbrick. 'This is where I shoot!'

'I refuse to believe the evidence of my own eyes,' said the Doctor. 'These creatures simply do not exist.'

It soon became clear, however, that this was the Llanabba Silver Band. 'Why, it's my friend the station-master!' said Philbrick as their leader came over to the Doctor.

'Three pounds you said you would pay us for playing.'

'Yes, yes, that's right, three pounds. There is a small tent for you, next to the tea-tent. Take your band in there!'

'We can play nothing whatever without the money first,' said the station-master.

'Shall I hit him on the ear?' offered Philbrick.

'No, no. You have not lived in Wales as long as I have.' The

Doctor took a wallet from his pocket, the sight of which seemed to fascinate the musicians. They crowded round him, making strange animal noises. 'There you are!' said the Doctor, handing three pounds to the leader. 'Now take your men into the tent and keep them there until after tea. Understand?'

The band crept away. 'The Welsh character is an interesting study,' said the Doctor to Paul. 'Let me tell you—' But he was interrupted by a breathless little boy, who ran up to inform them that Lord and Lady Circle had arrived.

Lady Circle was a large, elderly woman dressed in sensible, comfortable-looking clothes, with a deep voice and a powerful handshake. Her husband was tall and thin, with a long, fair moustache, and pale, watery eyes that reminded Paul a little of Mr Prendergast. The Doctor and his guests sat down on chairs close to the tea-tent. All the boys and masters were already on the playing-field.

'Who is that extraordinary man?' asked Lady Circle, pointing at Philbrick, who was still wearing his yellow jacket.

'He is the boxing expert and swimming professional,' said the Doctor. 'A finely developed figure, don't you think?'

'First race,' announced Paul, 'under sixteen. Starter, Mr Prendergast. From the tea-tent to the trees and back.'

'I shall say "Are you ready? One, two, three" and then fire,' said Mr Prendergast. 'Are you ready? One' – there was a loud bang. 'Oh dear! I'm sorry' – but the race had begun. Little Line was sitting on the grass crying, because he had been wounded in the foot by Mr Prendergast's bullet. Dusty took him into the tea-tent and gave him a large piece of cake, and very soon he was walking round again, although with some difficulty, and surrounded by a sympathetic crowd.

'A most unfortunate beginning,' said the Doctor.

'For God's sake, look after Prendy,' said Grimes in Paul's ear. 'He's completely drunk, and on only one whisky, too.' So while the next race was being run, Paul took Mr Prendergast by the arm and led him to the tea-tent.

'Dusty wants you to help her in there,' he said firmly, 'and for God's sake, don't come out until you feel better.'

By now the Clutterbucks had arrived. 'Didn't realize our boy could run so well!' said Mr Clutterbuck delightedly, after reading the programme. 'How's *your* young hopeful been doing, Lady Circle?' he added.

'My boy has been injured in the foot,' said Lady Circle coldly. 'He was shot at by one of the masters. No serious damage. But it is kind of you to ask.'

The races continued. Paul made the announcements, Philbrick fired his pistol, and the boys ran obediently from the tea-tent to the trees and back. The visitors clapped as young Clutterbuck reached the finishing-line ahead of all the others.

'Well done!' cried the Clutterbucks.

'That boy cheated,' said Lady Circle. 'He only ran the distance five times. All the others ran six times. I counted.'

'How dare you suggest such a thing?' said Mrs Clutterbuck.

'We don't want any unpleasantness to spoil the afternoon,' said the vicar, who had joined the group of parents.

'He deliberately cheated, the little rat,' said Lady Circle. 'You needn't think I'm going to present a prize to him. I won't.'

The Doctor made a brave attempt to calm the situation, but despite this, things were not easy. Fortunately, however, just at this moment an enormous, luxurious grey-and-silver car rolled soundlessly on to the field. In three seconds the Doctor was at the

'He deliberately cheated, the little rat,' said Lady Circle.

side of the car. The door opened, and a tall young man in a well-cut grey coat climbed out. After him, like the first breath of spring in Paris, came Mrs Beste-Chetwynde – long silk legs, fur body, a tight little black hat, diamonds, and the famous high voice – 'I hope you don't mind my bringing Chokey, Dr Fagan? He's just crazy about sport.'

'Dear Mrs Beste-Chetwynde!' said Dr Fagan, pressing her glove. 'Dear, dear Mrs Beste-Chetwynde!' He was unable for a moment to find any words of welcome, because 'Chokey', although beautifully dressed, was black.

In the tea-tent, it became clear that Mr Prendergast had been drinking the champagne-cup. It was also evident that the general disagreement over Clutterbuck's recent win had not been forgotten. There were now two opposing groups; on one side the Circles, Line and the vicar, and on the other the Clutterbucks and the two or three parents who had already been offended by Lady Circle that day. In the middle stood Chokey and Mrs Beste-Chetwynde. The social success of the afternoon depended on them. With or without her black man, Mrs Beste-Chetwynde was a woman of great importance.

'So disappointing,' she was saying, 'that we've missed the sports. We had to keep stopping all the time to see the churches. Chokey just loves old churches, don't you, darling?'

'I sure do,' said Chokey.

'Are you interested in music?' asked the Doctor politely.

'Well, just you hear that, Baby,' said Chokey. 'Am *I* interested in music? I should say I am. Yes, sir!'

'Now, darling, you mustn't get excited. I'll take you over and introduce you to Lady Circle. He's just crazy about meeting lords and ladies, aren't you, my sweet?'

'I sure am,' said Chokey.

'I've got an American friend,' said Mr Clutterbuck to Grimes and Philbrick, 'who's told me a thing or two about black men. To put it bluntly, *they have uncontrollable passions.*'

'What a terrible thing!' said Grimes.

'You can't blame them, of course. It's in their nature.'

'I had such a strange conversation,' Lord Circle was saying to Paul, 'with the band-leader over there. He asked if I would like to meet his sister-in-law, and when I said, "Yes, I'd be delighted," he said it normally cost a pound but he could offer me a special price. What *can* he have meant?'

'Which of the English churches did you like best, Mr Chokey?' Lady Circle was saying.

'Chokey's not really his name, you know. The angel's called Sebastian Cholmondley.'

'Well,' said Mr Cholmondley, 'they were all fine, just fine. When I saw them, my heart just rose up and sang within me. I sure am crazy about history. You all think because we're black, we only care about jazz. Why, I'd give all the jazz in the world for just one little stone from one of your churches.'

'Oh, you angel! I could eat you up, every bit.'

'And is this your first visit to an English school?' asked the Doctor.

'First? No! I've been to them all, Oxford, Cambridge and the new ones too. That's what I like, see? I appreciate education and art. I read Shakespeare too. Ever read any?'

'Yes,' said the Doctor, 'as a matter of fact, I have.'

'My people – the black people of this world – are essentially artistic. We have the child's natural love of song and colour. You white people think the poor black man has no soul – but you're wrong! He loves Shakespeare and churches and old paintings the same as you do! Why don't you stretch out the hand of friendship to the poor black man, who's as good as you are?'

'My sweet, don't get excited. They're all friends here.'

'Is that so?' said Chokey. 'Should I sing them a song?'

'No, don't do that, darling. Have some tea. You can talk to the vicar about God. Chokey's crazy about religion, too.' As Chokey started talking to the vicar, Mrs Beste-Chetwynde turned to Lady Circle. 'I sometimes think I'm getting rather bored with black people,' she said. 'Are you?'

'I have never had the opportunity.'

'They are *so* serious! They require *such* a lot of effort.'

Conversation continued in the tea-tent until early evening, while the silver band went on playing.

———

As the last car drove away, the Doctor turned to his daughters, Paul and Grimes. 'A rather disappointing day,' he said. 'Nothing seemed to go quite right despite all our preparations. I am sorry Mr Prendergast had that unfortunate disagreement with Mrs Beste-Chetwynde's black friend. They seemed so angry, and it was only about some small detail of church architecture. I have never known Mr Prendergast so aggressive!'

'I didn't like Lady Circle's speech,' said Flossie. 'She was very nasty about the Clutterbuck family.'

'Do you know,' said Dusty, 'Mr Cholmondley asked me if I'd ever heard of a writer called Charles Dickens.'

'He asked *me* to go to Brighton with him for the weekend,' said Flossie, 'in a rather sweet way, too.'

'Florence, I trust you refused?'

'Oh, yes,' said Flossie sadly, 'I refused.'

———

Back in the Common Room, Paul and Grimes sat moodily in the two armchairs. The room felt cold and cheerless.

'Well, old boy, so that's over,' said Grimes. 'As a party, I have known better. Old Prendy made rather a fool of himself, didn't he? You feeling all right, old man? You're a bit quiet.'

'I say, Grimes, what do you suppose the relationship is between Mrs Beste-Chetwynde and that black man?'

'Well, I don't suppose it's his fascinating conversation that attracts her. No, I imagine it's a simple case of good old sex.'

'Yes, I suppose you're right. She's invited me to visit her in London, you know.'

'Oh, you should go. She moves in the best social circles. There are photographs of her in all the papers.'

'I expect she looks good in photographs,' said Paul.

Grimes looked at him narrowly. 'Yes, not bad. Why are you suddenly so interested?'

'Oh, I don't know, just wondering.' They sat smoking for some time in silence. 'If Beste-Chetwynde is fifteen, that doesn't necessarily make her more than thirty-one, does it?'

'Old boy, you're in love.'

'Nonsense!'

'Love's young dream?'

'No, no.'

'A trembling hope?'

'Certainly not.'

'A sweet despair?'

'Nothing of the sort.'

'You're lying!' said Grimes. There was another pause.

'Grimes, I wonder if you can be right?'

'Sure of it, old boy. Just you go in and win. Good luck! May all your troubles be little ones!'

That night when Paul went to bed, he was struggling with feelings completely new to him.

5
THE SUFFERING OF CAPTAIN GRIMES

Next day Mr Prendergast looked considerably less cheerful.

'Head hurting?' asked Grimes. 'Feeling thirsty?'

'Well, yes, as a matter of fact.'

'Poor old Prendy! I know the feeling well! Still, it was worth it, wasn't it?'

'I don't remember very clearly all that happened, but I did have an interesting talk with Philbrick, who told me all about his life. It appears he is really a rich man and not a butler at all.'

'I know,' said Paul and Grimes at exactly the same time.

'You both knew? Well, it came as a great surprise to me to find he is really Sir Solomon Philbrick, the ship-owner.'

'The author, you mean,' said Grimes.

'The retired burglar,' said Paul.

The three masters looked at each other.

'Old boys,' said Grimes, 'it seems to me that someone's been playing a little game with us.'

'Well, this is the story he told me,' continued Mr Prendergast. 'As an extremely wealthy ship-owner, he attended all the best parties in London, with a lovely actress as his companion. One evening, however, after a card-game, he was challenged to a fight, and shot the other man dead. He was overcome by such a sense of guilt that he sent the actress away, and stayed alone in his deserted house, in the depths of misery. Finally he went to a priest and confessed. He was told that for three years he must give up his house and wealth, and live among the lowest of the low. That,' said Mr Prendergast simply, 'is why he's here. Wasn't that the story he told you?'

'No, it wasn't,' said Paul.

'Nothing like it at all,' said Grimes. 'He told me all about himself one evening at the pub. Apparently his father made a lot of money out of diamonds. There were two children, young Philbrick and a daughter called Gracie. From the start Philbrick was the old man's favourite, and had the best of everything, while Gracie lived with the servants downstairs. When the old man died, Philbrick inherited the whole fortune, and was so busy writing books that he didn't bother about his sister. Finally, desperate for some money, Gracie became a cook in a private house, and next year she died. That didn't worry Philbrick at first, but after a while he began to notice a horrible smell of cooking all over his house. He tried rebuilding the house, but the smell got worse. He tried going abroad, but the whole of Paris smelt of English cooking. Then he realized it must be Gracie's ghost. He decided that if he could live among servants for a year and write a book about them that would improve their living conditions, the ghost might leave him alone. So he came here.'

Paul told them about the *Lamb and Flag* in south London. 'Do you think that story's true, or yours, or Prendy's?'

'No,' said Mr Prendergast.

Two days later Beste-Chetwynde and Paul were having their organ lesson in Llanabba village church.

'I don't think I played that terribly well, do you, sir? Shall I stop for a bit?'

'I wish you would.'

'Line's foot has swollen up and turned black.'

'Poor little boy!' said Paul.

'I had a letter from my mother this morning. There's a

message for you in it. Shall I read you what she says?' He took out a letter written on the thickest possible paper. 'The first part is all about horse-racing and the quarrel she's had with Chokey. Apparently he doesn't like the way she's rebuilt our country house. I think it's time she gave him up, don't you?'

'What does she say about me?' asked Paul.

'She says: *"By the way, dear boy, I must tell you your spelling has become too terrible for words. You know how anxious I am for you to do well at school and go to university, so I've been thinking, might it be a good thing if we had a private teacher for you in the holidays? Someone young who would join in socially. I wondered if that good-looking young master you said you liked would care to come? I don't mean the drunk one, although he was sweet too."* I think that must be you, don't you? It can hardly be Captain Grimes.'

'Well, I must think it over,' said Paul. 'It sounds rather a good idea.'

'Well, yes,' said Beste-Chetwynde doubtfully, 'it might be all right, only there mustn't be too much of the schoolmaster about it.'

'And there'll be no organ lessons either,' said Paul.

Grimes did not receive the news as enthusiastically as Paul had hoped. He was sitting in the Common Room, miserably biting his nails.

'Good, old boy! That's wonderful,' he said absently. 'I'm glad for you, I am really.'

'Well, you don't sound exactly cheerful.'

'No, I'm not. The fact is, I'm in the soup again.'

'Badly?'

'Right up to the neck. Couldn't be worse.'

'My dear chap, I *am* sorry. What are you going to do?'

'I've done the only thing possible. I've announced my engagement.'

'That'll please Flossie.'

'Oh, yes, she's as pleased as hell about it.'

'What did the old man say?'

'It's puzzled him a bit, old boy. He's just considering things at the moment. Well, I expect everything'll be all right.'

'I don't see why it shouldn't be.'

'Well, there *is* a reason. I don't think I've told you before, but the fact is, I'm married already.'

That evening the Doctor sent for Paul. He was looking worried and old. 'Pennyfeather,' he said, 'I have this morning received two unpleasant shocks. The first was not unexpected. Your colleague, Captain Grimes, appears to be guilty of a crime which I can neither understand nor excuse. I need give no details. I have frequently met with similar cases during a long experience in our profession. But what has disturbed and saddened me more than I can express is the information that he is engaged to my elder daughter. I had not expected such shame to descend on my family. I could have forgiven him his wooden leg, his lack of money, his dishonesty and his ugly face, if only he had been a *gentleman*. Pennyfeather, what I wished to say to you was this: I have spoken to my unfortunate daughter and find she has no particular liking for Grimes. Indeed, I do not think any daughter of mine could sink as low as that. But for some reason she is uncontrollably eager to get married to somebody fairly soon. Now, I would be prepared to offer a partnership in the school to a son-in-law of whom I approved. My partner would start at an income of a thousand, and of course inherit a larger share upon my death. Many young men would find this an inviting offer. And I was wondering, Pennyfeather, whether by any chance, looking at the matter from a business-like point of view, taking things as they are for what they are worth, you understand, whether possibly *you* . . .? I wonder if I make myself clear?'

'No,' said Paul. 'No, sir, I'm afraid it would be impossible. I hope I don't appear rude, but – no, really I'm afraid . . .'

'That's all right, my dear boy. I quite understand. Well, it must be Grimes, then. I don't think it would be any use asking Mr Prendergast. The wedding will take place a week today. You might tell Grimes that, if you see him. I want to have as little to do with him as possible.'

Paul returned to the Common Room with this message.

'Hell!' said Grimes. 'I still hoped it might not happen.'

'What do you want for a wedding present?' asked Paul.

Grimes began to look more cheerful. 'What about that party you promised me and Prendy?'

'All right!' said Paul. 'We'll have it tomorrow.'

The Hotel Metropole at Cympryddyg is by far the grandest hotel in the north of Wales. As Paul, Grimes and Mr Prendergast sat drinking their cocktails in the bar before dinner, they were surprised to see Philbrick enter. He appeared to be very much at home there, and was held in great respect by the waiters.

'Not a bad place, this,' he told them casually. 'I need a bit of luxury occasionally. You can't expect much in Wales. I'm not staying here for dinner, or I'd invite you all to eat with me.'

'Philbrick, old boy,' said Grimes, 'me and my friends here have been wanting a word with you for some time. How about those stories you told us about being a ship-owner and an author and a burglar?'

'Since you mention it,' said Philbrick calmly, 'they were untrue. One day you shall know my full story. It is stranger than anything you can imagine. Meanwhile, I have to be back at the Castle. Good night.'

They watched him leave the hotel, accompanied to his car by the manager, the head waiter, and the doorman.

Paul led his guests into the dining-room. A waiter advanced towards their table, bent under the weight of an enormous bottle of champagne. 'With best wishes from Sir Solomon Philbrick, sir, and congratulations to Captain Grimes on his approaching marriage, sir.'

'Well!' said Grimes. 'Good old Philbrick! Prendy, fill up your glass. Let's drink to Trumpington, whoever he is, who gave us the money for this little party!'

'And here's to Philbrick,' said Paul, 'whoever *he* is!'

'And here's to Miss Fagan,' said Mr Prendergast, 'with our warmest hopes for her future happiness!'

'Absolutely,' said Grimes. After their soup they had the worst sort of fish. Mr Prendergast made a little joke. Clearly the dinner-party was being a great success.

'You know,' said Grimes, 'however you look at it, marriage is rather an awful thought.'

'I must say I can't understand why the Church recommends it so highly,' agreed Mr Prendergast.

'My first marriage,' said Grimes, 'didn't really matter much. It was in Ireland. I was drunk at the time, and so was everyone else. God knows what became of Mrs Grimes. But it seems to me that with Flossie life is going to be pretty tough. It's not at all what I would have chosen for myself. Still, I suppose it's the best thing that could have happened. I think I've just about come to the end of the schoolmastering profession. Now I need never worry about having to get another job. That's something. In fact, that's all there is. But I don't mind telling you, there have been moments in the last twenty-four hours when I've gone cold all over, at the thought of my future with her.'

'I don't want to depress you,' said Mr Prendergast, 'but I've known Flossie for nearly ten years now, and—'

'There isn't anything you can tell me about Flossie that I don't know already. I almost wish it was Dusty. I suppose it's too late now to change. Oh dear!' said Grimes despairingly, staring into his glass. 'Oh, God! Oh, God! To think that I have come to this!'

'Cheer up, Grimes. It isn't like you to be as miserable as this,' said Paul.

'Old friends,' said Grimes, and his voice shook with deep feeling, 'you see a man standing face to face with his punishment. Respect him even if you cannot understand. Those who live for worldly pleasure shall die of it. Who will pity me in that dark hell into which I must descend? I have boasted in my youth and held my head high and gone laughing on my way, careless of what might happen, but always behind me, unseen, stood cold-eyed Justice with his two-edged weapon.'

More food was brought. Mr Prendergast ate large quantities with enthusiastic appreciation.

'Oh, why did nobody warn me?' cried Grimes, at the height of his suffering. 'I should have been told. They should have warned me about Flossie, not about the fires of hell. I've risked *them*, and I don't mind risking them again, but they should have told me about marriage. They should have told me that at the end of that happy journey and path of flowers were the ugly lights of home, the voices of children, the closeness and confidence of family life.

But I dare say I wouldn't have listened. Our life is lived between two homes. We come out for a short while into the light, and then the front door closes. There's a home and family waiting for every one of us. We can't escape, no matter how hard we try. It's the seed of life we carry about in our bodies, each one of us unconsciously pregnant with desirable town or country residences. As individuals we simply do not exist. What makes two people want to build their horrible home and have children? What *is* birth?'

'I've often wondered,' said Mr Prendergast.

'Well, *I* have no desire in that direction. But Nature forces it upon us, and Nature always wins. Oh, God! Why didn't I die in my first awful home? Why did I ever hope I could escape?' Grimes continued to speak for some time in deep bitterness of heart. Then he became silent and stared at his glass again.

'I wonder,' said Mr Prendergast, 'if I could have just a little more of this very excellent chicken?'

'Anyway,' said Grimes, 'there won't be any children. I'll make sure of that.'

'It has always been a mystery to me why quite happy, normal people marry,' said Mr Prendergast. 'I can't see the smallest reason for it. Now I can understand it in Grimes' case. He has everything to gain by the arrangement, but what does Flossie expect to gain? Very little, if anything. But she seems more enthusiastic about it than Grimes. I don't believe that people would ever fall in love or want to be married if they hadn't been told about it. It's like abroad – no one would want to go there if they hadn't been told it existed. Don't you agree?'

'I don't think you can be quite right,' said Paul. 'You see, animals fall in love quite a lot, don't they?'

'Do they?' said Mr Prendergast. 'I didn't know that. How extraordinary! But then it is surprising what animals can be taught. Apparently there is a monkey at the zoo who juggles with an umbrella and two oranges.'

'I know what I'll do,' said Grimes. 'I'll buy a motor-bicycle.' This seemed to cheer him up a little. He took another glass of wine and smiled weakly. 'I'm afraid I haven't been following the conversation. What were we talking about?'

'Prendy was telling me about a monkey who juggled with an umbrella and two oranges.'

'Why, that's nothing. I can juggle with a huge great bottle and some ice and two knives. Watch!'

'Grimes, don't! Everyone is looking at you.'

The head waiter came over. 'Please remember where you are, sir,' he said, frowning at Grimes.

'I know where I am well enough,' said Grimes. 'I'm in the hotel my friend Sir Solomon Philbrick is thinking of buying. And I tell you this, old boy, if he does, the first person to lose his job will be you. See?'

But he stopped juggling, and Mr Prendergast ate two slices of chocolate cake undisturbed.

'The black cloud has passed,' said Grimes. 'Grimes is now going to enjoy his evening.'

6
THE PASSING OF A PUBLIC-SCHOOL MAN

Six days later the school was given a half-holiday, and soon after lunch Captain Edgar Grimes and Miss Florence Selina Fagan were married at the Llanabba village church. A slight injury to

Paul's hand prevented him from playing the organ. The Doctor, still pained and upset, did not attend the ceremony. Everybody else, however, was there except little Lord Line, whose foot was being amputated at a local hospital. Most of the boys welcomed the event as a pleasant change from their usual routine.

'I don't suppose their children will be terribly attractive,' said Beste-Chetwynde.

There were few wedding presents. The boys had collected some money and bought a silver teapot. The Doctor gave a cheque for twenty-five pounds. Mr Prendergast bought Grimes a walking stick – 'because he was always borrowing mine' – and Dusty generously gave a mirror, a desk diary and a silver vase.

The ceremony was completed without any problems, as Grimes' Irish wife did not arrive to prevent it. Flossie wore a brightly coloured dress and a hat with two pink feathers to

Captain Grimes and Flossie were married in the village church.

match. During the wedding, the vicar spoke very movingly on Home and Married Love.

'How beautiful it is,' he said, 'to see two young people setting out on life's path together! How much more beautiful to see them when they have grown to full manhood and womanhood coming together and saying "Our experience of life has taught us that *one* is not enough."'

Then they all returned to the Castle. The wedding trip had been postponed until the end of term, ten days later, and the arrangements for the first few days of Mr and Mrs Grimes' married life were a little uncomfortable. 'You must do the best you can,' the Doctor had said. 'I suppose you will wish to share the same bedroom. I would not object to your moving into the large room in the West Tower. It is a little damp, but I dare say Diana will arrange for a fire to be lighted there. Captain Grimes will have his meals with me in my dining-room, not with the boys. I do not wish to find him in my other rooms.'

Diana, who was being very generous about the whole business, put a bowl of flowers in their bedroom and lit a huge fire there.

That evening Grimes visited Paul in the Common Room. He looked rather uncomfortable in his evening clothes. 'Well, that's over, for tonight, anyway,' he said. 'The old man certainly makes sure he has a good dinner.'

'How are you feeling?'

'Not too well, old boy. The first days are always a bit difficult, they say, even in the most romantic marriages. My father-in-law is *not* what you might call easy. I suppose as a married man I oughtn't to go to the pub?'

'It might look strange on the first evening, mightn't it?'

'Flossie's playing the piano, Dusty's adding up the accounts, the old man's reading in his study. Don't you think we've got time for a quick one?'

Arm in arm they went down the familiar road. 'I'm buying the drinks tonight,' said Grimes. In the pub they met the silver band and their leader. 'They tell me you were married this afternoon?' said the station-master.

'That's right,' said Grimes.

'And you never wanted to meet my sister-in-law,' the Welshman continued sadly.

'Look here, old boy,' said Grimes. 'Just you shut up. This is not the moment to talk about that sort of thing. I'll buy you all some beer, all right?'

When the pub closed that night, they returned to the Castle. A light was burning in the West Tower.

'There she is, waiting for me,' said Grimes. 'Now it might be a very romantic sight to some men, a light shining in a tower window. I knew a poem about a thing like that once. I forget it now. I used to be awfully keen on poems when I was younger – love and all that. Funny how one grows out of that sort of thing.'

Inside the Castle he turned off the main passage. 'Well, good night, old boy! This is the way I go now. See you in the morning.' The door closed behind him, and Paul went to bed.

Paul saw little of Grimes during the next few days. They met at prayers and on their way to and from their classrooms, but the door that separated the school from the Doctor's rooms was also separating them. Mr Prendergast was smoking in the Common Room one evening when he suddenly said, 'You know, I miss Grimes. I didn't think I would, but I do. With all his faults, he was a very cheerful person.'

'He doesn't look as cheerful as he did,' said Paul. 'I don't believe life in the Doctor's family suits him very well.'

As it happened, Grimes chose that evening to visit them. 'Do you chaps mind if I come in a for a while?' he asked, with none of his usual confidence. They rose to welcome him. 'Sure you don't mind? I won't stay long.'

'My dear man, we were just saying how much we missed you. Come and sit down,' said Paul.

'Have some of my tobacco,' said Prendergast.

'Thanks, Prendy. I just had to come in and have a talk. I've been feeling pretty fed up lately. Married life is not all fun, I don't mind telling you. Flossie's not the problem – she's hardly any trouble at all. In a way I quite like her. She likes me, anyway, and that's the great thing. No, it's the Doctor. He's always laughing at me in a nasty kind of way. He makes me feel small – you know, talking to me the way Lady Circle talks to the Clutterbucks.'

'I don't expect he means to,' said Paul, 'and anyway I wouldn't bother about it if I were you.'

'That's the point. It *does* bother me. I'm beginning to feel he's quite right. I suppose I'm a pretty coarse sort of chap. I don't know anything about art, and I haven't met any grand people, and I don't wear expensive clothes, but up to now, none of that has worried me. I felt as good as anyone else, and I didn't care what anyone thought as long as I had my fun. And I *did* have fun, too, and what's more, I enjoyed it. But now I've lived with that man for a week, I feel quite different. I feel half ashamed of myself all the time. And I've come to recognize that nasty look he gives me in other people's eyes as well.'

'Ah, how well I know that feeling!' sighed Prendergast.

'I used to think I was popular among the boys, but you know

I'm not, and at the pub they only pretend to like me in the hope I'll buy them drinks. Another thing – I used to use French expressions sometimes in conversation. I never thought about it, but I suppose I haven't got much of an accent. Well, every time I say one of them now, the Doctor looks as if he's bitten on a bad tooth. So I have to think carefully before I say anything, to see if it might displease him. Old boy, it's been hell this last week, and it's worrying me. I'm beginning to feel I'm worthless. That man'll make me crazy before the term's over.'

'Well, there's only a week more,' was all that Paul could say to comfort him.

Next morning at prayers Grimes handed Paul a letter. Paul opened it and read:

My dear Grimes,

The other day at the sports you asked whether there was by any chance a job for you at the brewery. A post is now vacant which might suit you. We need a traveller to go round to various pubs and hotels to taste our beer, to make sure it is in good condition. The salary is two hundred a year with car and travelling expenses. If this attracts you, please let me know during the next few days.

Yours sincerely,

Sam Clutterbuck

'Just look at that!' said Grimes gloomily. 'God's own job, and mine, if I asked for it! If that had come ten days ago, my whole life might have been different.'

'You aren't thinking of taking it now?'

'Too late, old boy. The saddest words in the English language – too late.'

In the break between lessons Grimes said to Paul, 'Look here,

I've decided to take Sam Clutterbuck's job. Who cares about the Fagans!' His eyes shone with excitement. 'I won't say a word to them. I'll just leave. They can do what they like.'

'It's much the best thing you can do!' said Paul.

An hour later, at the end of morning school, they met again. 'I've been thinking over that letter,' said Grimes. 'I see it all now. It's just a joke.'

'Nonsense!' said Paul. 'I'm sure it isn't.'

'They must have heard about my marriage from young Clutterbuck. Why should they offer *me* a job like that, even if such a wonderful job exists?'

'My dear Grimes, I'm certain it was a serious offer. There's nothing to lose by going to see them.'

'No, no, it's too late, old boy. Things like that just don't happen.' And he disappeared behind the Doctor's door.

Next day there was fresh trouble at Llanabba. Two detectives arrived at the Castle to arrest Philbrick. The buildings and grounds were searched, but then it was discovered that he had already left on the morning train to Holyhead, and would probably be in Ireland that afternoon.

'Is it a very serious case?' asked Mr Prendergast. 'Not shooting or anything like that?'

'No, he hasn't spilt any blood yet, sir. Between you and me, I think he's a bit mad. He pretends to be a very wealthy man, you see, sir, stays at a big hotel for some time living like a lord, calling himself Sir Solomon Philbrick, then leaves without paying his bill. Been doing this all over the country. Funny thing is, I think he really believes his own story.'

'Well, anyway,' said Dusty, 'he went without his wages from here.'

'I always felt there was something unreliable about that man,' said Mr Prendergast.

'Lucky devil!' said Grimes miserably.

—————=◈=—————

'I'm worried about Grimes,' said Mr Prendergast that evening. 'I never saw a man more changed. He used to be so self-confident. He came in here quite nervously just now, and asked me whether I believed that God punished people in this world or the next. I began to talk to him about it, but I could see he wasn't listening. He sighed once or twice, and then went out without a word while I was still speaking.'

'Poor Grimes! It'll be a relief when the holidays start.'

But Captain Grimes' holiday came sooner than anybody expected. Three days later he did not appear at morning prayers, and Flossie, red-eyed, admitted that he had not come home from the village the night before. Some of the villagers said they had seen him in the pub, looking depressed. Just before lunch a young man arrived at the Castle, with a little pile of clothes he had found on the beach. They were identified without difficulty as the Captain's. In the jacket pocket was an envelope addressed to the Doctor, and in it a sheet of paper, on which was written:

THOSE WHO LIVE FOR WORLDLY PLEASURE
SHALL DIE OF IT.

This information was kept a secret from the boys, as far as possible. Flossie, although extremely shocked at losing her husband so early in her married life, was determined not to wear black. 'I don't think my husband would have expected it of me,' she said.

In these upsetting circumstances, the boys began packing their cases to go away for the Easter holidays.

Margot Beste-Chetwynde had two houses in England – one in London and the other in the country, in Hampshire. Her London house, which had stood for over two hundred years, was generally considered the most beautiful building between Bond Street and Park Lane, but opinion was divided on her country house. This was very new indeed; in fact, it was hardly finished when Paul went to stay there at the beginning of the Easter holidays. No single act in Mrs Beste-Chetwynde's eventful and in many ways shocking life had excited quite so much critical comment as the building, or rather the rebuilding, of this remarkable house.

It was called King's Thursday, and stood on the place where the ancient family of Pastmaster had always lived. Since the mid-sixteenth century the great house had been here, unchanged by any additions or improvements over the years. No rooms had been added, no windows filled in, no towers built, simply because the Pastmasters of three centuries had lacked both the money and the energy to carry out the work. Even when indoor toilets and gas heaters became wildly fashionable, King's Thursday slept on, untouched by modernization. Candles still lighted the bedrooms long after all Lord Pastmaster's neighbours had electricity.

In the last fifty years, Hampshire people had gradually become proud of King's Thursday. Hostesses often took their weekend visitors there for afternoon tea, as it was considered to be an unusually fine and unspoilt example of Tudor architecture. It was impossible to ring the Pastmasters up, as they were not on the telephone, but they were always at home and delighted to see their neighbours. After tea Lord Pastmaster used to take the visitors on a guided tour of the cold dark bedrooms and great empty halls. Later they drove away in their comfortable cars to their modernized homes, and as they sat in their hot baths before dinner, the more sensitive among them felt fortunate to have been able to step back for an hour and a half out of their own century into the past, and to experience life exactly as it was lived in Tudor times.

But the time came when King's Thursday had to be sold. When it was originally built, it had required twenty servants to do the daily work, and even now it was scarcely possible to live there with fewer than that. And servants, the twentieth-century Pastmasters discovered, were not at all eager to sleep in the tiny dark bedrooms under the roof, or cook on a smoky open fire, or run up and down stairs carrying heavy containers of hot water for the family's baths. Modern servants required lifts, and hot water taps, and gas cookers, and electric lights.

Less unwillingly than might have been expected, Lord Pastmaster made up his mind to sell the house. To tell the truth, he preferred to live in the south of France. But his neighbours in the Hampshire villages as well as in the great country houses, were horrified, and for several months the newspapers were full of worried letters and articles. The *London News* expert on architecture, Mr Jack Tower, wrote with great feeling that losing such a piece of English history would be disastrous, and recommended that it should be sold to the nation, for the public to enjoy in future. But not enough money was collected to pay the very high price which Lord Pastmaster was sensible enough to demand.

So the news that Lord Pastmaster's rich sister-in-law had bought King's Thursday was received with the greatest delight by everybody, as they all assumed she would keep the ancient house as it was. They did not know that Margot Beste-Chetwynde did not appreciate Tudor architecture. She had been to the place once before, during her engagement. 'It's worse than I thought, far worse,' she said when she visited it soon after the sale had been completed, and shook her lovely head impatiently as she remembered the romantic young girl she had been, many years before.

Mr Jack Tower was busily saving another historic building, Saint Stephen's Church in Egg Street, London, when he heard that Margot had decided to rebuild King's Thursday. He said, 'Well, we did what we could,' and thought no more about it. Her neighbours, however, became increasingly angry as the great house lost its roof, its chimneys, and then its walls, gradually becoming nothing more than a pile of stones. Margot's architect, Otto Silenus, a young man who called himself Professor, was already at work on plans for the new house. 'Something clean and square,' had been Mrs Beste-Chetwynde's instructions, and then she had disappeared on one of her mysterious world tours, saying as she left, 'Please make sure it is finished by the spring.'

Professor Silenus was not yet very famous anywhere, and those who met him had very different reactions to his clever ideas. 'The problem of architecture as I see it,' he told a journalist who had come to report on the progress of his surprising creation of metal and glass, 'is the problem of all art – the removal of humans from the consideration of design. The only perfect building must be the factory, because that is built to house machines, not people. I do not think it is possible for domestic architecture to be beautiful, but I am doing my best. All evil comes from mankind,' he said gloomily, 'please tell your readers that.'

'Lord's Sister-in-Law's Builder on Future of Architecture,' thought the journalist happily. 'Will Machines Live in Houses? Amazing Ideas of Professor-Architect.'

Professor Silenus watched the journalist drive away, and then, taking a sweet from his pocket, began to chew it.

'I suppose there ought to be stairs,' he said, sighing. 'Why can't the creatures stay in one place? Why can't they sit still and work? Do engines require stairs? Do monkeys require houses? What a childish, self-destructive, out-of-date thing man is! On one side we have the natural movements and balanced responses of the animal, and on the other the reliable performance of the machine, and between them, mankind, neither *being*, nor *doing*, only *becoming*!'

Two hours later, the workmen came to receive further orders from the Professor. He had not moved from where the journalist had left him; he was staring fixedly into space, and he was still chewing, although he had finished the sweet long ago.

8
PAUL IN LOVE

Arthur Potts knew all about King's Thursday and Professor Silenus.

As soon as Paul arrived in London at the beginning of the holidays, Potts rang him up and arranged to have dinner with him. They met at a restaurant where they had often eaten together before, and where they had discussed so many matters of public importance, like the nation's financial situation, birth control, and Italian art. For the first time since the disturbing events of the Bollinger dinner, Paul felt relaxed. Llanabba Castle School had faded into the mists of forgetfulness, like a bad dream. For an evening at least, Paul knew himself to be an intelligent, well-educated, well-behaved young man, who could be trusted to use his vote sensibly, whose opinion on a concert or a book was rather better than most people's, who could order dinner without embarrassment and in an acceptable French accent, who would not lose luggage at foreign railway stations, and who might be expected to deal with all the emergencies of civilized life with firmness and efficiency. This was the Paul Pennyfeather who had been developing in the uneventful years before this story. In fact, the whole of this book is really about the mysterious disappearance of Paul Pennyfeather, as he originally was, so that readers must not complain if the shadowy figure which took his name and his place in society does not satisfactorily fill the important part of hero in this book.

'I saw some of Otto Silenus's work in Munich,' said Potts. 'Very promising. He can't be more than twenty-five now. There were some photographs of King's Thursday in a paper the other day. It looked extremely interesting. It's said to be the only really *imaginative* building since the French Revolution.'

They continued discussing modern architecture. Then Paul told Potts about the death of Grimes and the doubts of Mr Prendergast. Potts told Paul about a rather interesting job he had got with the League of Nations, which meant that he had decided to give up his studies at Oxford.

For an evening Paul became a real person again, but when he woke up next day, his solidity had disappeared and the shadow had returned. His extraordinary adventures were about to start again. He met Beste-Chetwynde at Waterloo Station, and together they took a morning train down to Hampshire. Mrs Beste-Chetwynde's driver collected them from the village station in the Rolls Royce, and as they drove through the beautiful countryside, Paul was lost in admiration. New leaves on the great, ancient trees looked fresh and green in the warm April sunshine, and a distant blue lake was visible across the rolling parkland. 'The dreaming beauty of the English countryside,' he thought. 'Surely this represents something calm, something permanent, in a world which has lost its reason? Surely this will always be here, when the confusion and panic of modern life has been forgotten? Surely—' But suddenly his thoughts were interrupted. They had come into sight of the house.

'What an amazing place!' said Beste-Chetwynde.

The car stopped. Paul and Beste-Chetwynde got out and were led across a floor of bottle-green glass into the dining-room, where Mrs Beste-Chetwynde was already seated at the black rubber table, beginning her lunch.

'My dears!' she cried, putting out a hand to each of them. 'How heavenly to see you!'

She was a thousand times more beautiful than all Paul's feverish memories of her. He watched her, as if in a dream.

'Darling boy, how are you?' she said to her son. 'Do you know, you're beginning to look rather lovely? Don't you think so, Otto?'

Paul had noticed nothing in the room except Mrs Beste-Chetwynde. He now saw there was a young man sitting beside her, with very fair hair and large glasses, behind which his cold eyes lay like slim fish in a bowl.

'His head is too big and his hands are too small,' said Professor Silenus. 'But his skin is pretty.'

'Could I make Mr Pennyfeather a cocktail?' Peter asked.

'Yes, Peter, dear, do. He makes them rather well. You can't think how busy I've been this week, moving in and showing visitors and newspaper photographers round the house. It doesn't seem to be a great success with the neighbours, does it, Otto, darling?'

'They are right, of course,' said Otto. 'How glad I shall be when the house is finished and I can go!'

'Don't you like it?' asked Peter over the cocktail-shaker. 'I think it's so good. It was rather Chokey's taste before.'

'I hate every part of it,' said Professor Silenus gloomily.

'I hate every part of it,' said Otto Silenus gloomily.

'Nothing I have ever done has caused me so much disgust.' With a deep sigh he rose from the table and left the room, still holding the fork with which he had been eating.

'Otto has *such* original ideas,' said Mrs Beste-Chetwynde. 'You must be sweet to him, Peter. There are a whole lot of people coming tomorrow for the weekend, and, my dear, that Maltravers has invited himself again. You wouldn't like me to marry him, would you, darling?'

'No,' said Peter. 'If you must marry again, do choose someone young and quiet.'

'Peter, you're an angel. I will. But now I'm going to bed. Show Mr Pennyfeather round the house, darling.'

The steel lift went up, and Paul came down to earth. It was three days before he next saw Mrs Beste-Chetwynde.

That night after dinner, he and Professor Silenus were standing looking out of the long dining-room windows. Outside, the black glass columns shone in the moonlight.

'Don't you think she's the most wonderful woman in the world?' said Paul. 'The most beautiful and the most free, almost like a creature of a completely different type, not a human being at all. Don't you feel that?'

'No,' said the Professor, after a few moments' thought. 'I can't say that I do. Physically her body works in exactly the same way as other women's. If you compare her with other women of her age, you will see that the differences are tiny, just a few millimetres here and there. In fact, it is these small variations that I find so annoying in Margot. Otherwise I might marry her.'

'Why do you think she might marry you?'

'Because, as I said, she has normal physical needs. Anyway, she has asked me to marry her twice. The first time I said I'd think it over, and the second time I refused. I'm sure I was right. She would interrupt my work terribly. Besides, she's getting old. In ten years she'll be almost worn out.' He looked at his gold watch, a gift from Mrs Beste-Chetwynde. 'Quarter to ten. I must go to bed. What do you take to make you sleep?'

'I sleep quite easily,' said Paul, 'except on trains.'

'You're lucky. Margot takes sleeping pills. I haven't been to sleep for over a year. That's why I go to bed early. You need more rest if you don't sleep.'

That night as Paul switched off his light and lay down to sleep, he thought of the young man a few bedrooms away, lying quite still in the darkness, his eyes closed and his brain turning and turning regularly all night. And in another corner of this extraordinary house lay Margot Beste-Chetwynde in a drugged state, her lovely, sweet-smelling body cool and scarcely moving beneath the sheets.

During the next day, the weekend guests arrived at various times, but Mrs Beste-Chetwynde stayed in her room, while Peter received the visitors in the prettiest way possible. Paul never learnt all their names, nor was he ever sure exactly how many of them there were. The guests greeted each other with little cries of delight, and played music, and danced, and drank cocktails, and appeared irregularly at meals.

Only one of them seemed very different from the rest – Sir Humphrey Maltravers, the Minister of Transport. He was the only one of the cheerful little party who commented on the absence of their hostess.

'Margot? No, I haven't seen her at all. I don't think she's terribly well,' said one of them, 'or perhaps she's got lost somewhere in the house. Peter will know.'

Paul found the Minister sitting alone in the garden after lunch, smoking a large cigar, his big red hands folded over his large stomach, a soft hat over his eyes.

'Hullo, young man,' he said. 'Where's everybody?'

'I think Peter's showing them round the house. Would you care to join them?'

'No, thank you. I came here for a rest. I've been working damned hard lately. I can't think why I keep on at politics. It's a dog's life, and there's no money in it either. When you're over forty, you know, you appreciate rest – rest and wealth. And half your life is lived after forty. Remember that, young man. Have you known Mrs Beste-Chetwynde long?'

'Only a few weeks,' said Paul.

'There's no one like her. But why did she build this house? It's all because of these strange friends of hers. It's not good for her. Damned awkward situation to be in, a rich woman without a husband! She's bound to be talked about. What Margot ought to do is marry – someone who would regularize her position, someone,' said Sir Humphrey, 'with a position in public life.'

And then, without any apparent connection of thought, he began to talk about himself. Why was it, Paul wondered, that all the people he met wanted to tell him the story of their lives? He supposed he must have a sympathetic look about him.

Early on Monday morning, Paul and Peter watched on the front steps as the Minister of Transport's car rolled away.

'I rather think he expected to see Mother,' said Peter. 'What a lot he ate! I did my best to make him feel at home, too, by talking to him about trains.'

They went back inside to begin another spelling lesson.

As the last of the guests departed, Mrs Beste-Chetwynde

reappeared from her drugged sleep, fresh and beautiful as a love poem. The green glass seemed to burst into flower under her feet as she passed from the lift to the cocktail table.

'You poor angels!' she said. 'Did you have a hell of a time with Maltravers? And all those people? I gave up inviting people long ago,' she added, turning to Paul, 'but they still come. More and more I feel the need of a husband, but Peter is horribly choosy.'

'Well, your men are all so awful,' said Peter.

In the whole of Paul's life no one had ever been quite so sweet to him as Margot Beste-Chetwynde was during the next few days. He moved around the great house in a golden mist, and each morning as he dressed, a bird seemed to be singing in his heart.

'Paul, dear,' she said one day as hand in hand, after a rather fearful meeting with a swan, they reached the safety of the house, 'I can't bear to think of you going back to that awful school. Do please write and tell Dr Fagan that you won't.'

'I don't quite see what else I could do,' said Paul.

'Darling, I could find you a job.'

'What sort of job, Margot?' Paul watched the swan swimming calmly across the lake. He dared not look at Margot.

'Well, Paul, you might stay and protect me from swans, mightn't you?' She put a cigarette in her mouth, and Paul lit it for her. 'My dear, what an unsteady hand! I'm afraid you're drinking too many of Peter's cocktails. But seriously, I'm sure I can find you a better job. I still manage a great deal of my father's business, you know, mostly in South America, in – in places of entertainment, hotels, theatres, places like that.'

'Oughtn't I to know Spanish?' asked Paul.

Margot threw away her cigarette with a little laugh. 'Time to change for dinner. You *are* being difficult today, aren't you?'

Paul thought about this conversation as he lay in his bath, and all the time while he dressed and as he tied his tie, he trembled from head to foot like a toy moved by wires.

At dinner Margot talked about matters of daily interest. Later, when they were alone, she said, 'People talk a great deal of nonsense about the disadvantages of being rich. There *are* problems involved, but still, *I* wouldn't be poor for anything. Would you be happy if you were rich, do you think?'

'I think there's only one thing that could make me really happy,' said Paul, 'and if I got that, I'd be rich too, but it wouldn't matter being rich, because if I hadn't got what would make me happy, I wouldn't be happy even if I were rich, you see.'

'My darling, that's rather complicated,' said Margot, 'but I think it may mean something rather sweet. If it does, I'm glad.'

'Margot, darling, please, will you marry me?' Paul was on his knees by her chair, his hands on hers.

'Well, that's rather what I've been wanting to discuss with you all day.' But surely there was a tremble in her voice?

'Does that mean you just possibly might, Margot? Is there a chance that you will?'

'I don't see why not. Of course we must ask Peter about it, and there are other things we ought to discuss first,' and then, quite suddenly, 'Paul, dear, dear creature, come here.'

Later on, they went to find Peter in the dining-room.

'Peter, we've something to tell you,' said Margot. 'Paul says he wants me to marry him.'

'Wonderful!' said Peter. 'I *am* glad. I've been trying to arrange it all this week, in fact. I think it's an excellent idea.'

'You're the first man he's said that about, Paul.'

'Oh, Margot, let's get married at once.'

'My dear, I haven't said yes yet. I'll tell you tomorrow.'

'No, tell me now, Margot. You do like me a little, don't you? Please marry me just terribly soon.'

'I'll tell you in the morning. There are several things to think about first.'

That night Paul found it unusually difficult to sleep. Long after he had switched off his light, he lay awake, his thoughts racing uncontrollably. Suddenly he realized that his door was being quietly opened. He could see nothing, but he heard the movement of silk as someone came into the room.

'Paul, are you asleep?' The door was closed.

'Margot!'

'Quiet, dear! Don't switch on the light.' It sounded as if the silk was falling to the ground. 'It's best to make sure, isn't it, darling, before we decide anything? It may be just an idea of yours that you're in love with me. And you see, Paul, I like you so very much, it would be a pity to make a mistake, wouldn't it?'

But fortunately there was no mistake, and next day Paul and Margot announced their engagement.

Crossing the hall a few days later, Paul met a short man with a long red beard walking towards Margot's study.

'My God!' he said.

'Not a word, old boy!' said the bearded man as he passed. A few minutes later, Paul was joined by Peter. 'I say, Paul,' he said, 'who do you think's talking to Mother?'

'I know,' said Paul. 'It's a very strange thing.'

'I somehow never felt he was dead,' said Peter.

They managed to catch Grimes on his way out.

'In the soup again?' asked Paul.

'Well, not exactly, but things haven't been good lately. The police are looking for me. They don't believe I killed myself. My other wife appeared, so that made them suspect me. That's why I'm wearing a false beard. Good disguise, eh?'

They led him back to the house, where Peter mixed him an extremely strong cocktail. 'What we want to know,' said Peter, 'is why you've come to see Mother.'

'Well,' said Grimes, 'after I left Llanabba, I went to London, wondering what to do next. I was in a pub when Bill, an old friend of mine, recognized me and told me about a job he could help me to get. Bill had gone to Argentina and been employed as manager of a' – he hesitated – 'a place of entertainment. Sort of night club, you know. There are lots of them there, a whole chain of them, in fact. He'd come back to England to find a couple of chaps to help him. Had to be chaps who could control themselves where women were concerned. That's what made him think of me. Lucky we met in that pub, eh! Well, the business was originally started by young Beste-Chetwynde's grandfather, and Mrs Beste-Chetwynde still takes an interest in it, so I was sent down here for an interview with her. I never thought it was the same Mrs Beste-Chetwynde who came to the Sports Day! Small world we live in, eh?'

'Did Mother give you the job?' asked Peter.

'She did, and fifty pounds for expenses. It's been a good day for Grimes. Heard from the old man lately, by the way?'

'Yes,' said Paul, 'I got a letter this morning. Here it is.'

Llanabba Castle School, North Wales
My dear Pennyfeather,
Thank you for your letter. I need hardly tell you what a real disappointment it is to hear that you are not returning to us.

However, my daughters and I wish you every happiness in your married life.

The holidays have not been restful so far. We have been continually bothered by a most disagreeable young Irish woman, who claims to be the widow of poor Captain Grimes. The police, too, make frequent visits, asking indelicate questions about my unfortunate son-in-law. Besides this, I have had a letter from Mr Prendergast stating that he, too, wishes to resign his post. Apparently he intends to return to the Church, as there is now a new type of vicar, called a 'Modern Churchman', for whom religious belief is not a necessary qualification. This may be a comfort to him, but only adds to my own inconvenience.

Indeed, I hardly feel able to continue at Llanabba. I have had an offer from a cinema company, whose manager, strangely enough, is called Sir Solomon Philbrick; they wish to buy the Castle. My daughter Diana is anxious to start a nursing home or a hotel. So you see things are not easy.

Yours sincerely,
Augustus Fagan

There was another surprise for Paul that day. Hardly had Grimes left the house when a tall young man with thoughtful eyes arrived at the door. It was Potts.

'My dear chap,' said Paul, 'I *am* glad to see you.'

'I saw your engagement in *The Times*,' said Potts, 'and as I was in the area, I wondered if you'd let me see the house.'

Paul and Peter showed him round. He admired everything, but it was not this that he had come to see. As soon as he and Paul were alone, he said casually, 'Who was that little man I met who was just leaving?'

72

'I think he was something to do with the Society for the Preservation of Ancient Buildings,' said Paul. 'Why?'

'Are you sure?' asked Potts in evident disappointment. 'How maddening! I thought I'd found him this time.'

'Are you doing private detective work, Potts?'

'No, no, it's all to do with the League of Nations,' said Potts quickly, and went on to talk of other things.

Margot invited Potts to dinner. He tried hard to make a good impression on Professor Silenus, but in this he was not successful. In fact, it was probably Potts' visit which finally got rid of the Professor, who left early the next morning, without bothering to take any of his possessions with him, and was not seen at King's Thursday again.

9
BUSINESS IN SOUTH AMERICA

At the end of April Peter returned to Llanabba, as the Castle had not yet been sold, and Margot and Paul went up to London to make arrangements for the wedding. Even though she had been married before, Margot had decided to have a full church wedding, with white bridal dress, flowers everywhere, organ music, and a huge champagne reception for hundreds of guests afterwards. But before the wedding, she had a good deal of South American business to finish.

The work seemed to consist mainly of interviewing young women for jobs in bars and as dancing partners. With some unwillingness Margot allowed Paul to be present one morning, as she interviewed the next group of girls in her study.

Paul sat at one side, fascinated by Margot's business ability.

All her dreaminess had left her. She sat at her desk, looking cool and efficient, pen in hand. One by one, the girls were shown in.

'Name?' said Margot.

'Pompilia de la Conradine.'

'Real name?'

'Bessy Brown.'

'Age?'

'Twenty-two.'

'Experience?'

'I was at Mrs Rosenbaum's for two years, madam.'

'Well, Bessy, why did you leave Mrs Rosenbaum's?'

'She said the gentlemen liked a change, madam.'

'I'll just ask her.' Margot picked up the phone. 'Is that Mrs Rosenbaum? This is South American Entertainments Limited speaking. Can you tell me why Miss de la Conradine left you? . . . Oh, I see. I rather thought that might be the reason. Thank you.' She put the phone down. 'Sorry, Bessy, nothing for you.'

Another young lady was shown in.

'Name?'

'Jane Grimes. The gentleman in Cardiff gave me a note for you, madam.' She passed a dirty-looking envelope over to Margot, who took out the note and read it.

'Yes, I see. So you're new to the business, Jane? But you're married, aren't you?'

'Yes, madam, but it was in the war and he was very drunk. They say he's dead now.'

'That's excellent, Jane. You're just the sort we want. I'm sending two very nice girls to Rio de Janeiro at the end of the week. Would you like to go with them?'

'Yes, madam, I'd be very pleased, I'm sure.'

'I'll send you your tickets in a day or so.' Mrs Grimes went out, and another girl took her place.

By lunch-time Margot was tired. 'Thank God that's the last of them. Were you terribly bored, my angel?'

'Margot, you're wonderful. So good at business!'

'Do you know, there's a young man just like your friend Potts down in the street,' she said from the window. 'And, my dear, he's started talking to the last of those poor girls we saw.'

'Then it can't be Potts,' said Paul lazily. 'I say, Margot, there's one thing I didn't understand. Why was it that the less experience they had, the more you seemed to want them? You offered higher wages to those who'd never worked before.'

'Did I, darling? Probably because I feel so wildly happy.' They walked out to lunch in the sunshine. At the table next to theirs in the restaurant, drinking champagne, was Philbrick. Paul stopped to speak to him for a moment.

'The police came for you soon after you left,' Paul said.

'They're bound to get me one day,' said Philbrick, 'but thanks for telling me anyway! By the way, you might warn your future bride that they'll be taking an interest in her soon, if she's not careful. The League of Nations is getting busy at last.'

'I haven't the least idea what you mean,' said Paul.

'Obviously the poor man's mad,' said Margot when he rejoined her and told her of the conversation.

Meanwhile, half the shops in London were involved in the wedding preparations. Paul had asked Potts to be his best man, but Potts, writing from Geneva, had refused. Paul had no other friends he had known for a long time, but fortunately he had recently received so many letters and invitations from people he hardly knew that his only difficulty in finding another best man was the fear of offending any of his affectionate new friends. Eventually he chose Sir Alastair Digby-Vane-Trumpington, because he felt that, however indirectly, he owed him a great deal of his present good luck.

For some reason, the public seemed to consider Paul's marriage particularly romantic. Perhaps they admired Margot's bravery, in willingly suffering, after ten years of widowhood, the hundred and one horrors of a society wedding, or perhaps Paul's sudden rise from poor schoolmaster to wealthy husband appealed to them, as something that might happen to anyone, with luck. 'It may be me next time,' people said to themselves, in offices and factories all over the country. High society was less certain in its approval. Lady Circle said, 'It's maddening that Line's died, just at this moment. People might think that's my reason for refusing the invitation. I can't imagine *anyone* will go.' All the fashionable single men were shocked that such a prize had been stolen from them, but they accepted Margot's invitations despite their annoyance.

Ten days before the wedding, Paul moved into rooms at the Ritz Hotel, while Margot spent her time on serious shopping. Five or six times a day messengers appeared at the Ritz, delivering little presents for Paul. In addition, Margot had fixed his personal allowance at two thousand pounds a year. Far away on the island of Corfu, preparations were being made at Mrs Beste-Chetwynde's luxury villa, where Paul and Margot were going to stay immediately after the wedding.

However, there was a problem. Three days before the wedding, Margot rang Paul at the Ritz.

'Darling, rather an annoying thing's happened. You know those girls we sent to Rio the other day? Well, they're held up in

Paul moved into rooms at the Ritz Hotel.

Marseille, I don't know why. I wonder if you could be an angel and go over and fix things for me? It's probably only a matter of giving the right man a few hundred francs. If you fly, you'll be back in plenty of time. I'd go myself, only you know, darling, I simply haven't one minute to spare.'

Paul did not have to travel alone. Potts was at the airport. 'League of Nations business,' he said, and was sick twice on the flight.

Paul was beginning to feel quite a man of the world, the Ritz today, Marseille tomorrow, Corfu the next day. The whole world seemed to stand open to him like one great hotel. In Marseille he had dinner at the best restaurant, and then took a taxi to the old part of town, where Margot had said the girls were staying. After paying the driver and getting out, he suddenly realized how dark and dirty the narrow streets were. He hurried on, past a drunk sailor, who, waving a bottle, spoke to him in some unknown language, and past several young ladies in lighted doorways, whose invitations were only too easy to understand. No wonder, he thought, that Margot had been so anxious to rescue her girls from this place of temptation and danger. How typical of her, that in all her world of luxury, she still had time to care for the poor girls she had unknowingly put at such risk!

Deaf to the offers he was receiving on all sides, Paul went on walking. Suddenly a girl with bare legs took his hat from his head, and then appeared at a window, calling him to come in and get it back. All the street seemed to be laughing at him. He hesitated, and then in a moment of panic, giving up both his hat and his self-control, he turned and escaped to the wide, well-lit, civilized streets where he knew he was at home.

By daylight the old town had lost most of its terrors. Paul found Mrs Grimes and her two friends in the small hotel where they were staying, and then spent a tiring morning at police stations and government offices. Things were more difficult than he had thought, and the officials either received him with extreme coldness or strangely knowing smiles and jokes. 'Things were easier six months ago,' they said, 'but now, with the League of Nations—' and they looked at Paul despairingly. Eventually the young ladies were allowed to travel on a ship to Rio as waitresses, but it cost Paul several thousand francs to complete the arrangements. 'What a silly thing the League of Nations seems to be!' said Paul. 'They appear to make it harder to travel instead of easier!' And this, to his surprise, the officials took as a great joke.

Paul sent Margot a telegram which read: *Everything arranged satisfactorily. Returning this afternoon. All my love.* He then left by air, feeling that at last he had done something to help.

At ten o'clock on his wedding morning he arrived at the Ritz. It was raining hard, and he felt tired and unshaven. In his rooms he found Peter, already dressed for the wedding.

'They let me come up from Llanabba for the day. Do you like my suit? Pretty good, eh? I've ordered some champagne and some lunch for us. I say, Paul, you're looking tired.'

But when Paul had had his bath, shaved and dressed, he felt much better. Soon Alastair Digby-Vane-Trumpington came in, and they all drank some champagne before going down to lunch in the hotel restaurant. It gave Paul some satisfaction to notice that he was the centre of interest of the whole room. During the meal he was called away to the phone.

'Darling,' said Margot, 'how are you? I've been so anxious all the time you were away. I had an awful feeling something was going to stop you coming back. Yes, I'm terribly well. I can't tell you, my dear, how young and pure I feel. I hope you'll like my dress. Goodbye, my sweet.'

By two o'clock they had finished lunch, and Margot's second-best Rolls Royce was waiting outside the hotel.

'It's a funny thing,' said the best man. 'No one could have guessed that when I had the Bollinger party in my rooms at Scone College, it was going to end like this.'

Paul turned his brandy round in his glass, smelled its richness for a second, then held it up. 'To Lady Luck,' he said. 'She's been good to me!'

'Which of you gentlemen is Paul Pennyfeather?'

Paul put down his glass and turned to find an elderly man of military appearance standing beside the table.

'I am,' said Paul. 'But I'm afraid I really haven't time . . .'

'I'm Inspector Bruce, of Scotland Yard. Will you be so good as to speak to me for a minute outside?'

'Really, officer,' said Paul, 'I'm in a great hurry. I suppose it's about the policemen to guard the wedding presents, but—'

'It's not about presents. I am instructed to arrest you.'

'Look here,' said Sir Alastair, 'don't be a fool. You've got the wrong man. This'll make the chaps at Scotland Yard laugh at you like anything. You simply can't arrest him! This is the Mr Pennyfeather who's being married today.'

'All I know is that I have the documents for his arrest, and that anything he says may be used in evidence against him.'

'It's all some awful mistake,' said Paul. 'I suppose I must go with this man. Try and phone Margot to explain to her.'

Sir Alastair's pink face showed amazement. 'Good God! How damned funny! At least it would be, at any other time.' But Peter, deadly white, had left the restaurant.

———◆———

Paul's trial, which took place some weeks later, was a bitter disappointment to the public. The arrest at the Ritz, the postponement of the wedding, Margot's departure for Corfu, the meals sent in to Paul on covered dishes from London's best restaurants, had been front-page stories every day. After all this, the trial itself lacked excitement. Potts, as chief witness against Paul, was unshakeable, and was later warmly thanked by the court; no evidence, except of previous good behaviour, was offered by the defence; Mrs Beste-Chetwynde's name was not mentioned, although the judge remarked with disgust that 'just before his arrest for this most horrible and infamous of crimes, the accused had been preparing to marry and bring down to

his own pitiable level a lady of beauty and stainless reputation.'
The judge added sternly, 'Society is justly disapproving of those
who buy their pleasures in the market of humanity, but no
punishment is too heavy for those evil men who make financial
gain from providing such pleasures.' So Paul was sent to prison,
and the public lost interest in him.

Before the trial, however, a conversation took place in his cell.
Peter Beste-Chetwynde came to visit him.

'Hullo, Paul! Mother asked me to come and see you. Are you
getting the food she's ordered for you?'

'Yes, it's delicious,' said Paul. 'How is Margot?'

'She's gone off alone to Corfu. I made her go, although she
wanted to stay and see your trial. You can imagine what a
terrible time we've had with reporters and people. And listen,
there's something else. You remember that awful old man
Maltravers? You know he's Home Secretary now? He's been to
see Mother, and said that, as he's responsible for all the judges
and prisons and police and so on, he could get you out, *if* she
married him. Mother thinks it's probably true, and she wants to
know how you feel about it. She feels the whole thing's rather her
fault, really, and she'll do anything to help, except go to prison
herself. You can't imagine her in prison, can you? So, would you
rather get out now, and she'll marry Maltravers? Or wait until
you do get out, and then marry her yourself? She was rather
definite about wanting to know.'

Paul thought of the Professor's 'In ten years she'll be worn
out', but he said, 'I'd rather she waited if you think she possibly
can.'

'I thought you'd say that, Paul. I'm so glad! I don't suppose
you'll get more than a year or so, will you?'

'My God, I hope not,' said Paul. It was rather a shock to him to hear in court the next day that he would have to serve seven years with hard labour. 'In ten years she'll be worn out,' he thought as he was driven to Blackstone Prison.

10
PAUL IN PRISON

On his first day there, Paul met quite a number of people, some of whom he knew already. The first person was a prison warder with a distinctly threatening manner. He had evidently been reading the papers. 'Rather different from the Ritz, eh?' he said. 'We don't like your kind here, see? And we know how to treat them. You'll find that out, you dirty white slaver.'

The next person Paul met was Philbrick. His prison clothes fitted him badly, and he was unshaven, but there was still something of the grand manner about him. 'Thought I'd be seeing you soon,' he said. 'As I've been here before, I've been put in charge of the uniforms. I've been saving the best suit I could find for you. It's pretty clean, on the whole.' He gave Paul a little pile of clothes. 'You'll be sent to have a bath next.'

Paul sat for ten minutes in twenty-five centimetres of warm water, as the prison rules required, and then put on his uniform. His personal possessions were taken away from him; this gave him a curiously pleasant sense of irresponsibility.

Next he saw the Doctor, who asked, 'Have you at any time been locked up in a hospital or home for mad people?'

'I was at Scone College, Oxford, for two years.'

The Doctor looked up. 'Don't you dare to make jokes here, my man.'

'Sorry,' said Paul.

'Don't speak to the Doctor except to answer a question,' said the warder at his elbow.

'Sorry,' said Paul again, without thinking, and was banged on the head.

Then he was taken to his cell. His next visit was from the Schoolmaster. 'Can you read and write, D.4.12?'

'Yes,' said Paul.

'What was your level when you left school?'

'Well, I don't quite know. I don't think we had levels.'

The Schoolmaster wrote down 'Memory lacking' in his notes, and gave Paul a book. 'You must do your best with that for the next four weeks. You see, it begins there,' he added helpfully, showing Paul the first page. It was a book on the development and use of the English language, printed in 1872.

'Thank you,' said Paul politely. 'I'm sure I'll find it useful.'

Next came the Chaplain, who was new to the job. 'Do you wish to attend religious services? You must either attend all or none.' He spoke in a hurried, nervous manner.

'Hullo, Prendy!' said Paul.

'I didn't recognize you,' said Mr Prendergast. 'People look so alike in those clothes. This is most disturbing, Pennyfeather. Oh dear! It makes everything still more difficult!'

'What's the matter, Prendy? Doubts again?'

'No, no, discipline, my old trouble. Criminals are just as bad as boys, I find. They pretend to make confessions and tell me the most awful things, just to see what I'll say, and in chapel they laugh so much that the warders spend all their time correcting them. Please, Pennyfeather, if you don't mind, you mustn't call me Prendy, and if anyone passes the cell, will you stand up when you're talking to me? The Chief Warder has said some very stern things to me about discipline.'

At this moment a warder's face appeared at the small window in the cell door. 'I trust you realize the wickedness of your crime and the justice of your punishment?' said Mr Prendergast in a loud voice. 'Pray for forgiveness.'

'Sorry to disturb you, sir,' said the warder, 'but I've got to take D.4.12 to see the Governor.'

Sir Wilfred Lucas-Dockery had not been intended by nature or education to be a prison governor. He had been Professor of Social Sciences at a northern university, but his ambition to play a part in his country's public life was achieved when he was appointed Governor of Blackstone Prison.

He had his own ideas on how to manage a prison. 'You must understand,' he said to Paul, 'that it is my intention to make personal contact with each of the men in my care. I want you to take a pride in your prison and in your work here. What is this man's profession, officer?'

'The white slave trade, sir,' said the Chief Warder.

'Ah yes. Well, I'm afraid you won't have much opportunity for that here. What else have you done?'

'I was nearly a vicar once,' said Paul.

'Indeed? Well, I hope to get together a class for religious study eventually. But at the moment the Government rules are rather strict. For the first four weeks you'll have to stay alone in your cell, as the law requires. After that, we'll find you something more creative. I believe almost all crime could be prevented if people were allowed the freedom to express themselves artistically, and at last we have the chance of testing this. Have you any experience of art leather work?'

'No, I'm afraid not, sir.'

'Never mind. Do you read the *New Nation*, I wonder? There is a most pleasing article this week about our prison, called *The Lucas-Dockery Experiments*. I like the prisoners to know these things. It makes them feel proud of our achievements here.'

Paul was taken away. 'You can see,' said Sir Wilfred, 'what a difference it made to that unfortunate man, to know that he is part of this great social revolution.'

'Yes, sir,' said the Chief Warder, 'and by the way, two more prisoners have tried to kill themselves. You must really be stricter with them, sir. Those sharp tools you've allowed the men to use in the art leather class are just too tempting for them.'

———◆———

Paul looked round the cell where he was to spend the next four weeks. There was very little in it, apart from a bed, a chair and a table. He sat down on the hard, narrow bed, and fell into a kind of dream. It was the first time he had been really alone for months. How very refreshing it was, he thought.

The next four weeks were among the happiest of Paul's life. There were certainly few physical comforts, but at the Ritz Paul had learnt that physical comfort was not everything. It was so delightful, he found, to have absolutely no decisions to make, and no anxiety at all about what kind of impression he was making – in fact, to be free. Every morning a bell rang, and he got up and dressed. There was no need to shave, no hesitation about which tie to wear, none of the worries that occupy the waking moments of civilized man. Prisoners were expected to spend most of the day sewing postmen's bags, made of thick, coarse material, but Paul did not consider this difficult or unpleasant work, and he always finished his pile of bags early, so that his evenings were free for thinking and writing down the thoughts which had passed through his mind during the day.

Unusually for a prison governor, Sir Wilfred Lucas-Dockery possessed ambition, knowledge and a hopeful nature. He looked forward to a time when the Lucas-Dockery experiments would be recognized as the beginning of a new period in criminal treatment. His excellent qualities, however, did not prevent him from having many serious differences of opinion with the Chief Warder, whose views were more traditional.

'There's a request from D.4.12, sir. He's finished his four weeks on his own, and now he wants to know if he can stay alone for another four weeks.'

'I disapprove of that. Being alone for a long time makes a man inward-looking. Who is D.4.12?'

'Seven years with hard labour for involvement in the white slave trade, sir, waiting for transfer to Egdon Heath.'

'Bring D.4.12 in. I want to know why he wishes to give up the opportunity to be with other prisoners.'

Paul was led in, and explained, 'I find it so much more interesting, sir, working alone in my cell.'

'It's a most irregular suggestion,' said the Chief Warder. 'Put him in the observation cell, sir. That brings out any madness very quickly, even in a man who seems quite normal.'

But Sir Wilfred did not often take the Chief Warder's advice. He liked the prisoners to notice the difference between the official view and his own. 'I will consider your case, and give you my answer tomorrow,' he said.

Paul was led back to his cell, and next day appeared again in the Governor's office. 'I have considered your request with the greatest care,' said Sir Wilfred. 'In fact, I have decided to include it in the book I am writing on the criminal mind. I believe you are suffering from a fear of people, caused by your feelings of personal inadequacy in the presence of others. Therefore I shall attempt to break down your social reserve in the following way – you will take exercise for half an hour a day in the company of one other prisoner, talking about history, geography, public ceremonies, recent events and so on. I am sure you will be pleased to realize that individual attention is being paid to your case, which may in time attract international interest in the field of social sciences. That is something to lift you above the soul-destroying boredom of routine, isn't it?'

Paul was led away. That afternoon, his part in the Lucas-Dockery experiments began. He and another prisoner, a small, bony man, walked dutifully round the courtyard making conversation, during which Paul discovered that Philbrick had told the small man that he was Sir Solomon Lucas-Dockery, the Governor's brother. They walked together every day for a week, but then, for some reason, Paul found that his companion's place had been taken by a large, frightening-looking man, with red hair and beard, and red eyes, and huge red hands which kept opening and closing at his sides.

'How do you do?' said Paul politely. 'Are you here for long?'

'Life,' said the other, in a low, powerful voice. 'But it doesn't matter. I'm waiting for the end of the world to come. It'll happen any day now. Do you ever have visions? No, I can see you don't. Nor does the Chaplain. It was a vision that brought me here, an angel surrounded by flames, crying, "Kill, and spare no one." I didn't see his meaning at first, but suddenly it came to me! God had chosen me to kill for him! And so I killed God's enemy, I cut off his head, and now I'm in prison, but I will be saved when

87

Judgement Day comes, when God decides who among us will go to heaven or to hell!'

Paul complained to the Governor. 'I believe that the prisoner I have to take exercise with is a dangerous madman, sir.'

'Nonsense!' said the Governor. 'I myself chose that man; he is especially suitable. I wish to hear no more about this.'

That afternoon Paul spent another worrying half-hour in the courtyard.

'I've had another vision,' said the murderer. 'It was beautiful! The whole prison and all the warders were red and shining and wet with blood, in a great red lake. Then I woke up. I don't know the meaning of it yet, but I feel that God's hand is hanging over this prison. I sometimes dream of a great red tunnel, with men running down it, into the fires of hell. Do you?'

'I'm afraid not,' said Paul. 'Have they given you an interesting library book to read?'

'*Lady Dora's Secret*,' said God's chosen one. 'Too soft for me. I prefer the Bible. There's a lot of killing in that.'

'Oh dear, you seem to think about killing a great deal.'

'I do. It's my purpose in life, you see,' said the big man simply.

Next day a warder reported to the Governor that the red-haired prisoner had been singing religious songs and talking to himself excitedly in his cell. When told to keep quiet, he had answered extremely rudely. As usual, the Governor considered the case carefully, and was delighted to discover what he felt was the ideal solution. It was clear to Sir Wilfred that the poor man was suffering from an inability to express himself in his work. The Governor therefore gave orders that the prisoner should be given a number of woodwork tools, so that he could use his energy in a more positive and creative way.

Two days later, the prison was in a state of wild excitement. Something had happened. Perhaps, thought Paul, there was a disaster in the world outside – a war or revolution. The warders were obviously upset, but refused to explain why. Paul listened as two warders passed his cell door, talking.

'Well, I'm sorry for the poor chap. All I can say is, it was time the Governor had a lesson. It's all his fault.'

'It might easily have been one of us,' said the other in a shocked voice.

When breakfast arrived, Paul whispered eagerly to the prisoner serving the bread, 'What's happened?'

'Why, haven't you heard? There's been a murder.'

So the Governor had been murdered, thought Paul. He had been an interfering old fool. Still, it was disturbing news. He

Paul spent another worrying half-hour in the courtyard.

waited with scarcely controlled impatience for the daily service in the chapel. This was the only moment in the day when the prisoners could communicate easily; they were able to hold quite long conversations and pass on messages to each other, while pretending to sing the songs and say the prayers.

The prisoners marched in silence to the chapel, and by chance, Paul had the seat next to Philbrick. Paul looked round curiously. Clearly it was not the Governor who had been killed, as he was standing there in front of them. But where was Mr Prendergast? At last the organ started playing, and all over the chapel the men took a deep breath, filling their chests for several minutes of conversation.

'Oh God, our help in ages past,
'Where's Prendergast today?' sang Paul.
'Killed last night by a crazy chap
Who had some woodwork tools,' sang Philbrick.

'Who let the madman have the tools?'
'The Governor; who d'you think?
'The madman said he'd had a dream,
And cut off Prendy's head.'

'Beneath the shadow of God's house,
We shelter from the storm,
Damned lucky it was Prendergast,
Might have been you or me!'

From all points of view it was lucky that the madman had chosen Mr Prendergast to attack. If a prisoner or warder had been killed, a Home Office investigation would have been necessary, and this might have seriously discouraged the Lucas-

Dockery experiments. Mr Prendergast's death passed almost unnoticed. His killer was moved to another prison, and life at Blackstone went smoothly on. It was observed, however, that the Chief Warder seemed to have considerably more influence with Sir Wilfred than before. But Paul did not have time to appreciate this, because a few days later he was taken, with some others, to the prison at Egdon Heath.

11
PAUL SEES MARGOT AGAIN

Paul was being sent to Egdon Heath because his punishment involved hard labour, working in the quarries there. He travelled by train, with six other prisoners and two unusually friendly warders. One of them allowed Paul to read his newspaper, the first he had read for six weeks. He was deeply moved to discover, on the centre page, a dark but recognizable photograph of Margot and Peter. The article next to it reported that Margot's brother-in-law had died, and Peter Beste-Chetwynde had become the new Lord Pastmaster.

Paul sat back in his seat for a long time, looking at the photograph, while his companions played cards. So far he had failed to make up his mind about Margot. On one side was the still, small voice of the English gentleman; he had 'done the right thing' in protecting a woman, but Margot was certainly guilty, and he was sheltering her, not from misfortune or injustice, but from the consequence of her crimes. On the other side was the undeniable truth of Peter's words, 'You can't imagine Mother in prison, can you?' The more Paul considered this, the more he saw it as the statement of a natural law. There was, in fact, and

91

should be, one law for her, and another for everybody else. What did justice or the democratic system matter? It wasn't simply that Margot was very rich or that he was in love with her. It was just that he saw the *impossibility* of Margot in prison. If someone had to suffer, in order to prevent the public from providing poor Mrs Grimes with the only employment for which civilization had prepared her, then it had better be Paul, as anyone who has been to an English public school will always feel comparatively at home in prison.

How lovely Margot was, thought Paul, even in this poor photograph! Even his rough criminal companions noticed that there seemed to be a spring-like perfume in the compartment.

Paul found an old friend at Egdon Heath, a short, cheerful figure, who made a good deal of noise with his artificial leg. 'Here we are again, old boy!' he said, when they were working together, cutting stone in the quarries. 'I'm in the soup as usual. Been here a fortnight and it seems too long already. I've always been a sociable chap, and I don't like this. Three years is too long, old boy.'

'I suppose they discovered you had two wives?'

'Yes,' said Grimes. 'I should have stayed in South America. I was arrested as soon as I landed. But it was fun seeing poor old Flossie and my father-in-law in court. I hear the old man's shut down the school. Ever hear anything of Prendy?'

'He was murdered the other day.'

'Poor old Prendy! He didn't have a happy life, did he? Do you know, I think I'll give up schoolmastering for ever when I get out. It doesn't lead anywhere.'

'It seems to have led us both to the same place.'

Except for the work in the quarries, life at Egdon was almost the same as at Blackstone. After a week, however, Paul became conscious of a strange influence at work. First of all, the Chaplain came cheerfully into his cell, with a number of books under his arm. 'Your library books,' he said lightly, handing Paul two expensive new books, still in their plastic wrappers. 'Let me know if you'd like anything different. And if, by any chance, you're writing to Mrs Beste-Chetwynde, do mention that you think the prison library is good. She's paying for new seats in the chapel,' he added irrelevantly as he left.

Why does the Chaplain want me to mention the library to Margot? wondered Paul. But he liked the books.

Then, one evening, Paul returned from the quarries to find his cell heavy with perfume. His table was filled with a large bunch of winter roses, which had cost half a crown each in a London market that morning. At supper he often found some delicious speciality on his plate, while the other prisoners just had meat and potatoes. On another occasion the Doctor stopped at Paul's door, looked hard at him, and said, 'You need some medicine.' The next day a huge brown bottle was placed in Paul's cell, with instructions to take two glasses after each meal. Paul liked the medicine, because it was port.

Soon a letter came from Margot. It was not very long.

Dear Paul,

It is so difficult writing to you because, you know, I never can write letters, and it's so particularly hard with you because the warders read it and cross it all out if they don't like it. Peter and I are back at King's Thursday. Do you know, I don't really like this house terribly, and I'm having it rebuilt. Do you mind? Peter's become Lord Pastmaster – did you know? – and is rather sweet about it. I'm going to come and see you some time – may

*I? – when I can get away, but I have such a lot of things to do. I
do hope you're getting enough books and food and things, or will
they cross that out?*

Love, Margot

P.S. *I may be wrong, but I rather believe poor little Alastair
Trumpington's going to fall in love with me. What shall I do?*

Eventually Margot came herself. It was the first time they had
met since the morning in June when she had sent him off to rescue
her girls in Marseille. The meeting took place in a small room
used only for visitors. Margot sat at one end of the table, Paul at
the other, with a warder between them.

'I must ask you both to put your hands on the table in front of
you,' said the warder.

Margot laid her beautiful hands next to her gloves and bag.
Paul noticed for the first time how rough and coarse his hands
had become. For a moment neither of them spoke.

'Do I look awful?' Paul said at last. 'I haven't seen a mirror for
some time.'

'Well, perhaps a little, darling. Don't they let you shave?'

'No discussion of the prison system is permitted,' said the
warder. 'No complaints or negative comments are allowed.'

'Oh dear!' said Margot. 'This is going to be very difficult. I'm
almost sorry I came. You're glad I came, aren't you?'

'Don't mind me, madam,' said the warder kindly, 'if you want
to talk of personal things. I hear a good deal in this job, I can tell
you, and I keep it all confidential.'

'Paul, *do* say something, please,' said Margot.

'How's Alastair?'

'Rather sweet, really. He's always at King's Thursday now. I
like him.' Another pause. 'You know, Lady Circle simply

refused to speak to me the other day. I think some people no longer consider me respectable. Rather awful, isn't it?'

'How's business?' said Paul.

'Paul, you mustn't be nasty to me,' said Margot in a low voice. 'You wouldn't say that if you knew how I was feeling.'

'I'm sorry, Margot. Actually, I just wanted to know.'

'I'm selling the business. It's getting difficult in Rio.'

'Ten minutes more,' said the warder.

'Things haven't quite happened as we expected, have they?' said Margot. They talked about some parties she had been to, and the books he was reading. At last she said, 'Paul, I'm going. I just can't manage another moment of this.'

'It was nice of you to come,' said Paul.

'I've decided something rather important, just this minute. I'm going to marry Maltravers. I'm sorry, but I am.'

'I suppose it's because I look so awful?' said Paul.

'No, it's just everything. It's simply something that's going to happen. Oh dear! How difficult it is to say anything.'

'If you should want to kiss goodbye,' said the warder, 'it's not usual, as you aren't married. Still, I don't mind just once . . .'

'Oh, God!' said Margot, and left the room without looking back. Paul returned to his cell, greatly saddened at how little pain the afternoon's events had caused him.

Two days later, Grimes, the free spirit, made his escape from the prison. There happened to be a thick white fog over Egdon Heath, and Grimes took this opportunity to break away from the little group cutting stone in the quarries.

'Come back,' shouted the warder, 'or I'll fire!' He fired into the fog. 'He hasn't a hope,' he told the other prisoners. 'No one ever gets away for long. He'll be back, you'll see.'

But although all the neighbouring houses and farms were carefully searched, there was no sign of Grimes. It was assumed that he had fallen into a river and drowned, or died of hunger in a field, although his body was never found. A week later the Chaplain prayed for his soul, and the Governor informed the Home Secretary that Grimes was dead.

'What a horrible death,' said the Chaplain, 'dying alone like that.'

'Poor old Grimes!' said Paul. 'And he was a public-school man too.' But later, thinking things over as he peacefully ate the delicious supper provided for him, Paul knew that Grimes was not dead. Lord Line was dead; Mr Prendergast was dead; the time would even come for Paul Pennyfeather, but Grimes was a life force, and would rise again some time, somewhere, shaking the dust of the grave from his bones.

A few days later Paul was informed that he was being sent to a private nursing home to have a small operation. He was extremely surprised, as he knew no operation was necessary, but it seemed impossible to convince the Governor of this. He was given back his clothes, and allowed to shave, so that when he left the prison, with a warder, he looked like a normal, civilized man. The warder was polite, indeed almost respectful, towards him, and paid for their train tickets and lunch, including cigars, from a fat bundle of notes he was carrying. It was all very mysterious. They eventually arrived at a large house on the coast, in Worthing, Sussex, where the warder said, 'Dr Fagan's in charge now. Goodbye,' and left.

Dusty, dressed as a nurse, greeted Paul at the front door, without appearing to recognize him, and took him upstairs to a small room. Soon footsteps approached, and Dr Fagan, Sir

Alastair Digby-Vane-Trumpington, and an elderly little man came in. Paul still had no idea what was going on.

'Sorry we're late,' said Sir Alastair, 'but I've had an awful time with this man, trying to get him out of the pub. I was afraid he was too drunk to do the job, but I think he can just carry on. Have you got the papers ready?'

'Here they are,' said Dr Fagan. 'They state that an operation was carried out on the patient, Paul Pennyfeather, but that he died while still unconscious.'

'Poor old chap!' said the little doctor, and two tears of sympathy rolled down his face. 'It's a hard world, isn't it?'

'Don't worry,' said Sir Alastair. 'You did all you could.'

'This is the ordinary death certificate,' said Dr Fagan. 'Would you mind signing it?' The little doctor signed, bringing the legal life of Paul Pennyfeather to an end.

'Excellent!' said Sir Alastair. 'Now here's your money. If I were you, I'd go and have a drink while the pubs are still open.'

'Do you know, I think I will,' said the little doctor, and left the room. There was silence for nearly a minute. The presence of death, even in its coldest and most legal shape, seemed to create an air of gloom. This was broken by the arrival of Flossie, dressed in her usual bright colours.

'Why, here you all are!' she said with delight. 'And Mr Pennyfeather too! Quite a little party!'

She had said the right thing. The word 'party' produced an enthusiastic response from Dr Fagan. 'Supper is waiting for us downstairs,' he said. 'We will have some wine with it. I am sure we all have a great deal to be thankful for.'

After supper he made a little speech. 'I think this is an important evening for most of us, most of all for my dear friend and former colleague, Paul Pennyfeather, in whose death tonight we are all involved in some way. It is the beginning of a new period in his life, and in mine too, as this evening's events have made it possible for me to give up this nursing home, which has not been a success. I shall start again, and I think,' he said, looking at his daughters, 'that it is time I was alone. Let us raise our glasses and drink to Lady Luck – she has been good to us.'

Once before Paul had drunk to Lady Luck. This time there was no disaster. They drank silently, and then Alastair and Paul left the nursing home. They walked down to the sea together. A rowing boat was waiting for them on the beach, and in the distance was a large, luxury sailing boat.

'That's Margot's boat,' said Alastair. 'It'll take you to her villa at Corfu. You can stay there until you've decided what to do next. I've got to drive back to King's Thursday now. Margot will be anxious to know how things have gone. Good luck!'

'Goodbye,' said Paul. He got into the boat and was rowed away. Sir Alastair watched until he was out of sight.

12
BACK TO OXFORD

Three weeks later, Paul was sitting in the garden of Margot's villa, with his evening cocktail in front of him, watching the sun sink into the sea. It was odd being dead. That morning he had received from Margot a bunch of newspaper articles about himself, together with all his possessions, which had been sent to her from Egdon. He began to feel the need to talk to someone, to convince himself that he existed, and stepped out through the garden gate into the street. It was odd being dead.

On his way across the village square, he suddenly saw a familiar figure approaching.

'Hullo!' said Paul.

'Hullo!' said Otto Silenus. He was carrying a shapeless bag on his back. 'I suppose you're staying with Margot.'

'I'm staying at her house. She's in England.'

'That's a pity. I hoped I'd find her here. Still, I'll stay for a while, I think. Will there be room for me at the villa?'

'I suppose so. I'm alone here, apart from the servants.'

'I've changed my mind. I think I *will* marry Margot now.'

'Too late, I'm afraid. She's married someone else.'

'I never thought of that. Oh well, it doesn't matter really. Who did she marry? That sensible Maltravers?'

'Yes. He's called Lord Metroland now.'

'What a funny name!' They walked back to the villa together. 'I thought they sent you to prison.'

'Yes, they did, but I got out.'

'Yes, you must have, I suppose. Wasn't it nice?'

'Not terribly.'

'Funny! I thought it would suit you so well. You never know with people, do you, what's going to suit them?'

Margot's servants did not seem surprised at the arrival of another guest. After dinner Professor Silenus said, 'I think I'll stay a long time. I have no money left. Are you leaving soon?'

'Yes, I'm going back to Oxford to continue my religious studies. That's why I'm growing a moustache. I don't want people to recognize me, you see.'

'I think it makes you look uglier. Well, I must go to bed. I've only slept twice since I last saw you – that's about my average.' But instead of leaving, he walked to the window and looked out at the sea. 'It's a good thing for you to become a vicar,' he said at last. 'People get all the wrong ideas about life. They're mostly far too romantic. Shall I tell you about life?'

'Yes, do,' said Paul politely.

'Well, it's like the big wheel at an amusement park. You know? You pay your money and go into a room with rows of seats all round, and in the centre the floor is made of a great circle of shiny wood that turns very fast. At first you sit down and watch the others. They're all trying to sit in the wheel, and they keep falling off, and that makes everybody laugh. It's great fun.'

'That doesn't sound much like life,' said Paul sadly.

'Oh, but it *is*. You see, the nearer you can get to the central point of the wheel, the slower it moves, and the easier it is to stay on. Of course, at the exact centre, there's a point completely at rest, if only we could find it – that's where I myself want to be. Lots of people just enjoy jumping on and falling off and jumping on again. Then there are others, like Margot, who like sitting out as far as they can, holding on tightly. But the whole point about the wheel is that you needn't get on it at all, if you don't want to. It doesn't suit everyone.

'Now, you're a person who was clearly meant to stay in your seat, and if you get bored, watch the others. Somehow you got on to the wheel, and you were thrown off at once with a hard bump. It's all right for Margot, who can hold on, and for me, at the centre, but *you* must stay still in one place.'

He turned back from the window. 'I know of no more boring and useless activity than generalizing about life. Did you understand what I was saying?'

'Yes, I think so.'

'I think I'll have my meals alone in future. Will you tell the servants? It makes me feel quite ill to talk so much. Good night.'

'Good night,' said Paul.

———◦❦◦———

Some months later Paul returned to Oxford after an absence of little more than a year. After passing the entrance examination, he entered Scone College once more, wearing a thick moustache. This and his natural shyness created such a complete disguise that nobody recognized him. He kept the name of Pennyfeather, explaining to the Chaplain that he believed he had had a distant cousin at Scone a short time ago.

'He came to a very sad end,' said the Chaplain, 'a wild young man. Would you believe it, he used to take off all his clothes and dance in the courtyard at night!'

'He was a *very* distant cousin,' said Paul quickly.

'Yes, yes, I'm sure he was. You're not at all like him.'

Paul made a new friend, a quiet, serious student called Stubbs. As term went on, Paul and Stubbs went for walks in the countryside, visited ancient churches and drank tea together.

Paul rejoined the League of Nations Union. On one occasion he and Stubbs went to the local prison to visit the criminals there and sing songs to them. 'It opens the mind,' said Stubbs, 'to see all sides of life. How those unfortunate men appreciated our singing!'

One day, as Paul and Stubbs were walking to the library, they were nearly run down by an open Rolls Royce that swung round the corner at a dangerous speed. In the back sat Philbrick, expensively dressed. He waved a gloved hand to Paul as he passed. When Stubbs asked who it was, Paul said it was an author he knew, and Stubbs was rather impressed.

———◦❦◦———

It was Paul's third year of uneventful residence at Scone. Stubbs finished his drinking chocolate, and rose to return to his own rooms. 'That was an interesting talk this evening about the Polish voting system,' he said.

'Yes, wasn't it?' said Paul. Outside there was a confused shouting and breaking of glass. 'It seems the Bollinger are enjoying themselves. Whose rooms are they in, this time?'

'Pastmaster's, I think. Well, good night, Paul.'

'Good night,' said Paul. He put the cake tin away, refilled his pipe, and sat back comfortably in his chair.

Soon he heard footsteps and a knock at his door. Peter Beste-Chetwynde, Lord Pastmaster, came into the room. He was dressed in the bottle-green and white evening coat of the Bollinger Club. His face was red, and his dark hair untidy.

'May I come in? Have you got a drink?'

'You seem to have had quite a few already.'

'I've had the Bollinger in my rooms. Noisy crowd. Oh, hell! I must have a drink.'

'There's some whisky in the cupboard. You're drinking rather a lot these days, aren't you, Peter?'

Peter said nothing, but poured himself some whisky. 'Feeling a bit ill,' he said. Then, after a pause, 'Paul, why have you been ignoring me all this time?'

'I don't know. I didn't think there was much point in our knowing each other.'

'You're not angry about anything?'

'No, why should I be?'

'Oh, I don't know. *I've* been rather angry about the whole thing, you and Margot and the man Maltravers and everything.'

'How's Margot?'

'She's all right. D'you mind if I have another drink? Lady Metroland! What a name! What a man! Still, she's got Alastair all the time. Metroland doesn't mind. He's got what he wanted. I don't see much of them really. What do you do now, Paul?'

'I'm studying to enter the Church.'

'Wish I didn't feel so damned ill. You know, Paul, I think it was a mistake you ever got mixed up with us, don't you? We're different somehow. Don't think that's rude, do you, Paul?'

'No, I know exactly what you mean.'

'Funny thing – you used to teach me once, do you remember? And the organ, do you remember?'

'Yes, I remember,' said Paul.

'And then Margot Metroland wanted to marry you, do you remember?'

'Yes,' said Paul.

'And then you went to prison, and Alastair – that's Margot's

'I'm studying to enter the Church,' said Paul.

young man – and Metroland – that's her husband – got you out, do you remember?'

'Yes,' said Paul, 'I remember.'

'And here we are talking to one another like this, here, after all that! Funny, isn't it?'

'Yes, it is, rather.'

'Paul, do you remember what you said once at the Ritz – Alastair was there – that's Margot's young man, you know – do you remember? You said, "To Lady Luck, she's been good to me." Do you remember that?'

'Yes,' said Paul, 'I remember.'

'Good old Paul! I knew you would. Let's drink to that now, shall we? How did it go? Damn, I've forgotten it. Never mind. I wish I didn't feel so ill.'

'You drink too much, Peter.'

'Oh, damn, what else is there to do? You're going to be a vicar, Paul? Damned funny, that. You ought never to have got mixed up with me and Metroland. May I have another drink?'

'Time you went to bed, Peter, don't you think?'

'Yes, I suppose it is. Didn't mind my coming in, did you? After all, you used to teach me the organ, do you remember? Thanks for the whisky!'

Then Peter went out, and Paul relaxed back into his comfortable armchair to continue his serious reading. So, certain religious groups used to turn towards the ancient city of Jerusalem when they prayed. Interesting, thought Paul, as he made a note of the fact. Then he turned off the light and went into his bedroom to sleep.

GLOSSARY

amputate to cut off an arm or a leg in a medical operation

angel *(expression of affection)* sweet one, darling

apparent obvious, clearly seen or understood

architecture the design or style of a building

architect *(n)* a person who designs buildings

best man a male friend or relative of a bridegroom, who assists him at his wedding

Bible (the) the holy book of the Christian religion

boxing *(n)* fighting with fists, as a sport; **box** *(v)*

brewery a building where beer is made

bursar a person who manages the finances of a school or college

butler the chief male servant in a large house

cell a small room for one or more prisoners in a prison

champagne an expensive French white wine with bubbles in it

chap *(informal)* a man or a boy

chapel a small building or room for religious services

chaplain a priest who works in a school, college, or prison

cocktail an alcoholic drink made by mixing spirits, juices, etc.

common *(adj)* showing a lack of good taste, regarded as typical of the lower classes

common room a sitting-room for teachers at schools, colleges, etc.

damn *(informal)* an exclamation of annoyance

damned *(informal)* extremely, very

dean the head of a university college or department

don a lecturer or teacher at a college or university

fine *(n)* money to be paid as a punishment

fireworks paper containers of chemicals that burn or explode, with bright lights and loud noise

franc the unit of money in France

gentleman a man who always acts in an honourable way

get on with to have a good or friendly relationship with

gloom a feeling of sadness or depression; **gloomily** *(adv)*

guardian someone who is legally responsible for a young person
whose parents are dead

half a crown a coin worth 2.5 shillings before 1971 (now 12.5
pence)

Home Secretary the British government minister in charge of
home affairs, e.g. the police and the prisons

indecent offending against accepted moral standards

juggle *(v)* to throw a set of objects in the air and catch them
repeatedly, keeping one or more in the air at the same time

labour (hard labour) hard physical work

League of Nations Union a university society supporting the
League of Nations, which was an international organization
working towards world peace

organ a musical instrument like a large piano, played in church

panic *(n)* a sudden feeling of great and uncontrollable fear

port a strong, sweet, usually dark red wine made in Portugal

public school a private, usually residential, school for pupils
whose parents pay for their education

quarry a place where stone is dug out of the ground

romantic of love or idealistic feelings

Scotland Yard the main office of the London police, especially for
investigating crimes

send down to order a student to leave university because of bad
behaviour

shut up *(informal)* to stop or make somebody stop talking

sister/son/father-in-law the sister/son/father of a person's
husband or wife

sleeping pill   a pill containing a drug that helps people to sleep
soup (land in the soup) *(informal)*   to get oneself into trouble
starting-pistol   a gun fired to give the signal for the start of a race
sure *(informal, especially American)*   certainly
swan   a large, graceful, usually white bird with a long thin neck
telegram   a message sent by telephone and delivered in printed
  form
term   a period of several weeks during which classes are held at
  schools, universities, etc.
Tudor *(adj)*   a period of English history (1485–1603); the
  architectural style of that time
vicar   a priest in the Church of England
villa   a large house by the sea, etc., where people stay on holiday
warder   a person who works as a guard in a prison
Welsh   of Wales, its people or its language
white slave trade   the business of providing women to be used
  for sex
wig   false hair

Before Reading

1 Read the story introduction on the first page, and the back cover. *Decline and Fall* is a satirical novel. Bearing that in mind, what do you expect of the story? Circle Y (Yes) or N (No) for each idea.

1 The author will paint a realistic picture of the society of the time. Y/N

2 Oxford University and private schools will be shown as wholly admirable institutions. Y/N

3 The characters will be true to life, and should be taken seriously. Y/N

4 'Black humour' means showing sad, terrible, or shocking things in a way that is intended to be amusing. Y/N

2 What do you think might happen to Paul, and how might the story end? Choose some of these ideas.

1 Paul uses his teaching experience to start his own private school, and makes a fortune out of it.

2 Paul marries a rich and fashionable woman, who persuades him to commit a serious crime.

3 Paul makes a number of friends, all of whom desert him when he needs their help.

4 Paul learns a lot about different levels of society, but becomes a bitter and unhappy person.

5 Paul's adventures lead to his dishonour and death.

6 Paul's amazing experiences leave him largely unchanged.

While Reading

Read Chapters 1 and 2. Who said this, and to whom? What or who were they talking about?

1 'We shall have a week of it, at least.'
2 'Here's an awful man wearing the Bollinger tie.'
3 'It is certainly not acceptable behaviour.'
4 'I expect you'll become a schoolmaster, sir.'
5 'You shouldn't be too modest.'
6 'Well, you must do the best you can.'
7 'I usually get into the soup sooner or later.'
8 'It was all very pleasant until my *Doubts* began.'

Read Chapters 3 and 4. Are these sentences true (T) or false (F)? Rewrite the false sentences with the correct information.

1 In his first lesson Paul bribed the boys to make them behave.
2 Paul's first week was much worse than he had expected.
3 Alastair Digby-Vane-Trumpington had offered to give Paul £20 as an apology, and Arthur Potts urged Paul to accept it.
4 Paul was actually very pleased about Grimes' telegram to Potts.
5 Preparations for the Sports Day went on for several weeks.
6 Philbrick told Paul he had been a school butler all his life.
7 Grimes deliberately shot himself in the foot with the starting-pistol.
8 Mrs Beste-Chetwynde accused Lady Circle's son of cheating.
9 Paul only realized he had fallen in love with Peter's mother when Grimes suggested the idea to him.

Before you read Chapter 5 (*The suffering of Captain Grimes*), can you guess the answers to these questions?

1 Will Mr Prendergast be dismissed for getting drunk?
2 Will Lady Circle remove little Lord Line from the school?
3 Will Paul see Mrs Beste-Chetwynde again?
4 Will Grimes and Philbrick announce their engagements?
5 How do you think Captain Grimes will suffer?

Read Chapters 5 to 7. Choose the best question-word for these questions, and then answer them.

What / Who / Why

1 . . . claimed to be a ship-owner, an author, and a retired burglar?
2 . . . suggested a holiday job for Paul?
3 . . . was Grimes worried about his engagement to Flossie?
4 . . . would Dr Fagan have preferred as a son-in-law?
5 . . . was Mr Prendergast's opinion of marriage?
6 . . . did Grimes dislike most about his new life as a husband?
7 . . . offered Grimes employment at a brewery?
8 . . . did two detectives arrive at the school?
9 . . . happened to Grimes just before the Easter holidays?
10 . . . had Mrs Beste-Chetwynde done that so shocked her neighbours?

Before you read Chapter 8 (*Paul in love*), what do you think is going to happen? Circle Y (Yes) or N (No) for each possibility.

1 Margot soon tires of Paul and sends him away. Y/N
2 Paul proposes marriage to Margot and she accepts. Y/N
3 Peter disapproves and tries to prevent their marrying. Y/N
4 Paul decides that Margot is unworthy of his love. Y/N

Read Chapters 8 and 9, and answer these questions.

1 What was Peter's advice to his mother about remarrying?
2 Why didn't Otto Silenus accept Margot's offer of marriage?
3 Who, apart from Paul, was hoping to marry Margot?
4 Why was Captain Grimes wearing a false beard when he visited King's Thursday?
5 What was the nature of Margot's South American business?
6 Why did Paul have to fly to Marseille just before the wedding?
7 What part did the League of Nations and Arthur Potts play in Paul's downfall?
8 Why was Margot's name never mentioned during Paul's trial?

Before you read Chapters 10 to 12, what do you think will happen to all the characters? Choose some of these ideas.

1 In prison Paul meets Philbrick, Prendergast, and Grimes.
2 Paul is released early from prison, and marries Margot.
3 When Paul gets out of prison, he takes on a new identity and returns to Oxford to continue studying for the Church.
4 Dr Fagan plays a part in Paul's escape from prison.
5 Paul is sent to Australia to serve his prison sentence, and returns to Oxford University as an expert on the criminal mind.
6 Margot marries Maltravers, but also takes a lover.
7 Margot marries Maltravers, poisons him, and then marries Paul.
8 Otto Silenus rebuilds Margot's house in Corfu, and is her constant companion for the next ten years.
9 Captain Grimes is last heard of in Rio de Janeiro.
10 Mr Prendergast becomes a prison chaplain and is brutally murdered by a mad prisoner.

After Reading

1 Here are the thoughts of five characters at different points in the story. Which characters are they, and who or what are they thinking about? What has just happened in the story?

1 'I think I've got him now. I must keep a close eye on him when we land at Marseille. Why on earth does he look so relaxed? He obviously doesn't realize we're on to him! Wish I didn't feel so awful! Oh God, where's that bag? . . .'

2 'What a good-looking young man! I wonder if he's the master that darling Peter said he liked. Isn't he *sweet*? And if I'm not mistaken, he's looking over here in my direction. Perhaps he'd be interested in a little holiday job at King's Thursday . . .'

3 'How awful! I *knew* something like this would happen! Well, the wedding's off now, of course. I must ring Mother and tell her to start packing at once. She'll have to leave the country – she really mustn't get involved in all this.'

4 'There they go, off down to the beach. A most satisfactory evening's business for all of us. Just a little paperwork, to help a dear friend and colleague start a new life. And such a generous payment – mustn't mention the dear lady's name, of course.'

5 'Right, now what shall I put? Keep it simple, that's the thing. I'll have to use his name, of course, but he won't mind. I'm sure he'll thank me for it when he sees the cheque. I might suggest a little party when it arrives . . .'

2 Here are some extracts from Peter's diary, written while Paul was
   in prison. Choose one suitable word to fill each gap.

... On Mother's behalf I sent a _____ off today to Egdon Heath, to
_____ for the new seats in the _____, as well as two new books
_____ be delivered every week to Paul's _____. At least poor Paul
will have _____ to read now ...

... Mother says I _____ spend what I like on Paul, _____ I intend
to do exactly that, _____ it was our fault he was _____ to prison.
He'll be getting special _____ at supper nearly every day, and
_____ will be winter roses to greet _____ tonight, after his day in
the _____. Was rather pleased with myself for _____ of port. I
know he likes _____, and if it's put in a _____ bottle, the other
prisoners probably won't _____ he's getting special treatment! ...

... Mother's just _____ me she's decided to marry that _____
Maltravers – I can't believe it! She _____ to visit Paul today and it
_____ that the visit didn't go too _____. However, Maltravers
promised to get Paul _____ of prison, so tomorrow we're all _____
at the Ritz to discuss the _____ way to do it. Alastair suggests
_____ a doctor to sign a death _____ for Paul ...

3 The author explains to us (page 62) that Paul is not the usual kind
   of story 'hero', but more of a 'shadowy figure', a victim of events.

If Paul had been a more usual 'hero', what might he have done ...
   1 when told he was being sent down for indecent behaviour?
   2 when his guardian refused to allow him any money?
   3 when Margot asked him to do some business for her?
   4 when he was arrested and put on trial?
   5 when he was a free man again after his escape from prison?

4 **When Paul returned to Scone College, perhaps Mr Sniggs was curious about the previous student called Pennyfeather. Complete Paul's side of his conversation with Mr Sniggs.**

SNIGGS: Tell me, Pennyfeather, what happened to that distant
    cousin of yours – the one you mentioned to the Chaplain?
PAUL: _____
SNIGGS: Never heard of it. Somewhere in Wales, I suppose. Is he
    still there?
PAUL: _____
SNIGGS: Beste-Chetwynde? The chap who's now Lord Pastmaster?
PAUL: _____
SNIGGS: You mean Mrs Beste-Chetwynde? Good heavens! What a
    very lucky young man!
PAUL: _____
SNIGGS: Why ever not? Ah, just a minute, I remember – wasn't
    there a trial of some sort? Some unpleasant business?
PAUL: _____
SNIGGS: Dear, dear. That *is* bad. Found guilty, was he?
PAUL: _____
SNIGGS: He must have been given a good long prison sentence for
    that! Do you ever write to him in prison?
PAUL: _____
SNIGGS: Dead, eh? How sad. Still, he does seem to have had quite
    an interesting life, if rather a short one.

5 **Write a short paragraph about each of these characters, describing how their paths crossed Paul's. Use the notes to help you.**

* CAPTAIN GRIMES : Llanabba / marriage / drowned / arrested / Egdon Heath / escape

- PHILBRICK : butler / school / wild stories / arrest / hotels / paying his bills / Blackstone Prison / expensively dressed / Rolls Royce / Oxford
- MR PRENDERGAST : vicar / *Doubts* / teacher / Llanabba / control / prison chaplain / discipline / murdered / prisoner
- SIR ALASTAIR DIGBY-VANE-TRUMPINGTON : student / Scone College / Bollinger Club / drunken / trousers / £20 / apology / best man / wedding / arrangements / 'death' / lover
- ARTHUR POTTS : solid / reliable friend / Scone College / the League of Nations / the white slave trade / followed / Marseille / witness / trial
- DR AUGUSTUS FAGAN : owner / Llanabba / partnership / daughter / nursing home / minor operation / large bribe / Paul's 'death'
- PETER BESTE-CHETWYNDE : boy / Llanabba / organ lessons / mother / country house / spelling / trial / imprisonment / best possible treatment / Lord Pastmaster

6 **Do you think *Decline and Fall* is a good title? Why, or why not? Would any of these titles be better? Give your reasons.**

High Society	A Little Knowledge
In the Soup	Born a Gentleman
A Changed Man	The Bollinger Experience
Oh, Wicked World!	The Rise and Fall of Paul Pennyfeather

7 **Evelyn Waugh wrote in his Author's Note to *Decline and Fall*, 'Please bear in mind that IT IS MEANT TO BE FUNNY.' Did you find the book amusing? Why, or why not?**

ABOUT THE AUTHOR

Evelyn Arthur St John Waugh (1903-1966) was born in London, and educated at a public school and Oxford University. After Oxford he became a teacher in various private schools, but he did not enjoy the work, and he was dismissed from one school for drunkenness. He then moved on to journalism, and in 1928 published his first and hugely successful novel, *Decline and Fall*, which was based on his teaching experience. A second novel, *Vile Bodies*, followed two years later, and during the 1930s he established himself as England's leading satirical novelist with *Black Mischief*, *A Handful of Dust*, and *Scoop*. These novels, and *Put Out More Flags* in 1942, caught the witty and irresponsible mood of upper-class life in the 1920s and 30s.

In 1930 Waugh had become a Roman Catholic, and one of his most popular titles, *Brideshead Revisited* (1945), was a more serious novel about an aristocratic family with a long Catholic tradition. He used his experiences from the Second World War, during which he served as an officer in the Royal Marines, for three linked novels, later published as the trilogy *Sword of Honour* in 1965. The main character is Guy Crouchback, an honourable man who finds the modern world a difficult place to deal with. Even closer to the author's personal experiences is *The Ordeal of Gilbert Penfold* (1957), a fascinating account of a middle-aged writer's nervous breakdown.

There is a popular television version of *Brideshead Revisited*, and also a film based on *A Handful of Dust*. However, *Decline and Fall* remains a firm favourite with many readers, for its black humour and its biting satire on British education.

ABOUT BOOKWORMS

OXFORD BOOKWORMS LIBRARY
Classics • True Stories • Fantasy & Horror • Human Interest
Crime & Mystery • Thriller & Adventure

The OXFORD BOOKWORMS LIBRARY offers a wide range of original and adapted stories, both classic and modern, which take learners from elementary to advanced level through six carefully graded language stages:

Stage 1 (400 headwords)	**Stage 4** (1400 headwords)
Stage 2 (700 headwords)	**Stage 5** (1800 headwords)
Stage 3 (1000 headwords)	**Stage 6** (2500 headwords)

More than fifty titles are also available on cassette, and there are many titles at Stages 1 to 4 which are specially recommended for younger learners. In addition to the introductions and activities in each Bookworm, resource material includes photocopiable test worksheets and Teacher's Handbooks, which contain advice on running a class library and using cassettes, and the answers for the activities in the books.

Several other series are linked to the OXFORD BOOKWORMS LIBRARY. They range from highly illustrated readers for young learners, to playscripts, non-fiction readers, and unsimplified texts for advanced learners.

Oxford Bookworms Starters   *Oxford Bookworms Factfiles*
Oxford Bookworms Playscripts   *Oxford Bookworms Collection*

Details of these series and a full list of all titles in the OXFORD BOOKWORMS LIBRARY can be found in the *Oxford English* catalogues. A selection of titles from the OXFORD BOOKWORMS LIBRARY can be found on the next pages.

Jeeves and Friends

P. G. WODEHOUSE

Retold by Clare West

What on earth would Bertie Wooster do without Jeeves, his valet? Jeeves is calm, tactful, resourceful, and has the answer to every problem. Bertie, a pleasant young man but a bit short of brains, turns to Jeeves every time he gets into trouble. And Bertie is *always* in trouble.

These six stories include the most famous of P. G. Wodehouse's memorable characters. There are three stories about Bertie and Jeeves, and three about Lord Emsworth, who, like Bertie, is often in trouble, battling with his fierce sister Lady Constance, and his even fiercer Scottish gardener, the red-bearded Angus McAllister . . .

Cold Comfort Farm

STELLA GIBBONS

Retold by Clare West

The farm lies in the shadow of a hill, and the farmyard rarely sees the sun, even in summer, when the sukebind hangs heavy in the branches. Here live the Starkadders – Aunt Ada Doom, Judith, Amos, Seth, Reuben, Elfine . . . They lead messy, untidy lives, full of dark thoughts, moody silences, and sudden noisy quarrels.

That is, until their attractive young cousin arrives from London. Neat, sensible, efficient, Flora Poste cannot *bear* messes (they are so *uncivilized*). She begins to tidy up the Starkadders' lives at once . . .

BOOKWORMS · CLASSICS · STAGE 6

Pride and Prejudice

JANE AUSTEN

Retold by Clare West

'The moment I first met you, I noticed your pride, your sense of superiority, and your selfish disdain for the feelings of others. You are the last man in the world whom I could ever be persuaded to marry,' said Elizabeth Bennet.

And so Elizabeth rejects the proud Mr Darcy. Can nothing overcome her prejudice against him? And what of the other Bennet girls – their fortunes, and misfortunes, in the business of getting husbands?

This famous novel by Jane Austen is full of wise and humorous observation of the people and manners of her times.

BOOKWORMS · HUMAN INTEREST · STAGE 6

Dublin People

MAEVE BINCHY

Retold by Jennifer Bassett

A young country girl comes to live and work in Dublin. Jo is determined to be modern and independent, and to have a wonderful time. But life in a big city is full of strange surprises for a shy country girl . . .

Gerry Moore is a man with a problem – alcohol. He knows he must give it up, and his family and friends watch nervously as he battles against it. But drink is a hard enemy to fight . . .

These stories by the Irish writer Maeve Binchy are full of affectionate humour and wit, and sometimes a little sadness.

From the Cradle to the Grave

Short stories by

EVELYN WAUGH, SOMERSET MAUGHAM, ROALD DAHL, SAKI,
FRANK SARGESON, RAYMOND CARVER, H. E. BATES, SUSAN HILL

This collection of short stories explores the trials of life from youth
to old age: the idealism of young people, the stresses of marriage, the
anxieties of parenthood, and the loneliness and fears of older
people. There is a wide variety of styles of writing, from black
humour and satire to compassionate and realistic observation of the
follies and foibles of humankind.

A Window on the Universe

Short stories by

RAY BRADBURY, BILL BROWN, PHILIP K. DICK,
ARTHUR C. CLARKE, JEROME BIXBY, ISAAC ASIMOV, BRIAN ALDISS,
JOHN WYNDHAM, ROALD DAHL

What does the future hold in store for the human race? Aliens from
distant galaxies, telepathic horror, interstellar war, time-warps, the
shriek of a rose, collision with an asteroid – the unknown lies
around every corner, and the universe is a big place. These nine
science-fiction stories offer possibilities that are fantastic,
humorous, alarming, but always thought-provoking.